COURAGE BY DARKNESS

by Jeri Massi

PEABODY
ADVENTURE SERIES

Bob Jones University Press, Greenville, South Carolina 29614

Courage by Darkness

Edited by Suzette Jordan

Cover and illustrations by Dana Thompson

©1987 by Bob Jones University Press
Greenville, South Carolina 29614

ISBN 0-89084-412-7
Printed in the United States of America

20   19   18   17   16   15   14   13   12   11   10   9   8   7

Contents

Contents

The Peabody Series
Derwood, Inc.
A Dangerous Game
Treasure in the Yukon
Courage by Darkness

Publisher's Note

Christian children, parents, and educators have already acknowledged the Peabody Series as something refreshingly new—an incorporation of high and gripping adventure with the realistic struggles of Christian youth today. The Peabody Series presents the adventures of the youth group from the First Bible Church of Peabody, Wisconsin. Some of the same characters appear in several of the books, but each adventure belongs to a different member of the group.

The characters in these books do not find quick solutions to their difficulties. Like all Christians, they struggle, misunderstand, lose ground, gain ground, and ultimately come to a better understanding of the Lord.

In this adventure, the focus is on Jean, the third Derwood. Dissatisfied with herself for being cowardly and fearful, she sets out on a campaign to increase her courage. Afraid, on the one hand, that the Lord won't send her an adventure and yet afraid that He will, Jean sets out with her family to her uncle's farm in Alabama. During her stay, she gradually realizes what courage is and what it is not. Most importantly, she comes to see the Lord's hand guiding her life.

Chapter One
Something New

It's just me—Jean.

Meet the third Derwood: short, nearsighted, afraid of everything, and too smart for her own good.

Maybe where you live there's a kid who never does anything wrong, gets straight *A*'s, and always knows her Bible verses for Sunday school. If you know a kid like that, then you know what happens. Every time there's a rainstorm, *that's* the kid who gets worms tossed in her hair. Every time there's a big snow, *that's* the kid who gets snowballed first. Every time *you* do something wrong, that's the kid whom your mother wants you to start hanging around with. That's me, and I know already that you'd rather not.

We are all born sinners, but I started going straight at a very young age.

Maybe you've already read about Jack and Penny. They try to do the right thing and always end up getting into trouble. Then they wind up heroes, somehow, and get their pictures in the paper. Or maybe you've read about Scruggs. He started out as a big bully, my *prime tormenter* in the neighborhood. Then after he got saved, he became a lot more serious about things. I guess—next to me—he's the most serious person I know. He's serious about catching up in school; he's serious about going to church with his foster mother, Mrs. Bennett, and he's serious about proving to people that he's really changed. The only thing he's not serious about is me. He calls me "two-bit" and "half pint," and once I caught him trying on my glasses for Jack. The two of them thought that was very funny.

I suppose that the greatest trial of my short life has been Annette. She lives in Peabody, too—right in the same neighborhood as me, in fact—and she goes to my church. And even though she's a whole year older than I am, my parents and her parents think that we were cut out for each other. We always end up getting thrown together at every church picnic, ice cream social, three-legged race, and sing-along. I guess people think we ought to be friends because Annette and I seem a lot alike. She always gets straight A's, and she always knows her Bible verses, too. The only difference people see between us is that I'm just normal-looking, and she's pretty.

But Annette likes to do things that I don't like to do. For one thing, whenever report cards come out, she's always going around saying, "I got an A in math; what did you get?" As for me, I'd rather not rub it in on people. I don't care what other kids get in math. I just wish some of the kids would let me get into the dodge-ball games or even Chinese jump rope.

When it rains and someone gets a worm on me, I just manage to wiggle it off, but no one throws worms at Annette because she jumps up and down and screams until she's hoarse and then goes right to the principal or to her mother, and everybody gets in trouble. But I just can't do that. I get embarrassed yelling and screaming, and if you tell on people all the time for little things, it's like being a baby.

Another thing about Annette is that she's always asking me about being adopted—which I am. My father adopted me when he married my mother after my real father died. I guess I never thought much about it—except I was glad it gave me the same last name as all my other brothers and sisters. Jack and Penny are my second father's real children; so of course they're Derwoods, and then there's me, and then there's Renee and Freddy and Marie, who are the children to both my mother and second father. So that makes them Derwoods too.

Anyway, I never care about being adopted or being a stepchild, because Jack and Penny are my mother's stepchildren, and we're used to being half-brothers and half-sisters to Renee, Freddy, and Marie. And nobody really cares at home. We're all just the same to each other.

But I get tired of it when Annette keeps harping on my being adopted.

Anyway, one Sunday morning after Sunday school, I thought that maybe I would stay in the classroom until Annette went by in the hallway. Then I wouldn't have to walk with her and listen to her. So I stayed really quiet by the back desks, and I saw her go past in the hallway, looking for me. You might wonder why I never just told Annette that I didn't want to be friends with her, but there are two reasons: for one thing, I'm a chicken, and for another, Annette would beg and bully and maybe even threaten to tell on me. Usually whenever she says she's going to tell on me, I'm not even sure what I've done. But I get scared; so I give in and do what she wants.

Anyway, just when I thought she might be gone, in walked Mrs. Bennett, who I guess was collecting all the lesson books or something. She almost missed me; then she stopped and tilted her glasses down on her nose to see me better and said, "Why, Jean, are you hiding from someone?"

I didn't want to lie; so I just nodded.

"Who?"

"Somebody," I said.

She sat down at one of the desks. "Has somebody been unkind to you? Is anybody picking on you?"

"No, I guess not." I looked down. You really couldn't say that Annette picked on me, not the way most people think of it.

"Come here," she said, not sternly. I walked up to her.

"I saw Annette out in the hall waiting for you," she told me. "Is that whom you're hiding from?"

I nodded. I figured I would get a lecture about being fair to my friends and being nice and all that, but Mrs. Bennett didn't say anything for so long that I looked up at her. Upstairs, the organ started playing. That meant fifteen minutes until church started.

Mrs. Bennett has graying brown hair and blue eyes. Her glasses are bifocals, but she looks over them more often than she looks through them, it seems. Maybe it's just because people are that much bigger than print; so she doesn't need them when she's talking to someone.

"Are you a little bit afraid of Annette?" she asked me.

"I guess so."

Then she hesitated, until at last she said, "I have a job for you to do for me."

"You do?"

"Yes. Every Sunday morning I want you to come report to me and help me gather the lesson books and tidy up the classrooms before church. It's a one-person job, and I've picked you because I know I can rely on you. Do you want to do that?"

I knew what it meant. It meant Annette couldn't come with me. Just Mrs. Bennett and I would pick up the books and straighten up. That meant I didn't have to be with Annette, and she couldn't tell me who missed their verses or show me her newest dress or talk on and on and on about whatever she talked about.

"Yes, I'd like to do that," I said.

"There's one condition."

"What is it?"

"I want you to tell your mother that you're a little afraid of Annette."

"Wouldn't that be babyish?"

"Not if it's true. And your mother can't guess that you don't like being with Annette all the time unless you tell her."

"Okay."

Then she smiled at me. "You know, with Jack and William (that's what she calls Scruggs) gone to the Yukon, it must be pretty dull at your house this summer."

"It seems like everything that's any fun always happens to them—or to Penny," I blurted.

"Do you think so?"

"Yes, but I guess it doesn't matter. I always get scared anyway. Nothing ever happens to me because I always run away."

"Did you know," she ventured after a slight pause, "that the knights of the Middle Ages and Renaissance were always supposed to give credit to the Lord whenever they met up with an adventure?"

"No." I didn't know how Mrs. Bennett knew either. It was hard to imagine her reading up on knights and jousts and things like that. Maybe Scruggs had read about them and told her.

"Yes. Those who had any faith always assumed that God had sent them whatever battle they had to fight or wall they had to scale. Maybe if you thought about things that way, you wouldn't be afraid."

"Maybe not. I'd like to try."

"Then maybe it's time to ask the Lord to send you an adventure."

I glanced at her to see if she might be teasing me, but Mrs. Bennett doesn't usually tease people. She stood up. "I think a little adventure might be the best thing for you, Jean. Well, we'd better get upstairs. Don't forget what I told you."

"I won't."

I followed her upstairs and ran and joined my family in their pew. And just before the service started, I quickly bowed my head and asked the Lord to send me an adventure and change me from being so afraid of everything.

Chapter Two
Watching for Adventure

The only thing that happened on Monday morning was that I told my Mom about Annette, and how I didn't like always having to be with her. I told her I was a little afraid of Annette, too.

"Afraid?" Mom asked. Mom's usually folding laundry at our house, especially on Mondays. It's the best time to catch her. For one thing, she's so picky about it that she usually doesn't make you help her, and for another, she likes to talk while she's doing it.

"What have you got to be afraid of Annette for?"

"Well—" I hesitated, because I knew if I told her that Annette had sometimes said she'd tell on me, my Mom would want to know what she would tell on me for. And I couldn't remember anything that I'd done. Then what would happen if Mom asked Annette? I might have done something terrible and forgotten all about it. Like the time I was spray painting a poster for school and accidentally spray painted Sherwood, our cat. (He'd been sleeping behind the poster.) Of course, I'd already told Mom and Dad about that. It was kind of hard to hide, since Sherwood's left side had been changed to Williamsburg blue.

Or—and this was a possibility—Annette might make up something super-colossal. And then how would I prove I had never done it? What if they believed her and not me?

"Well," I said again, "sometimes if I want to do something that Annette doesn't like, she says that she's going to tell on me."

"Tell what?" Mom asked.

"Well, I don't know. I can't remember doing anything. That's what scares me."

"Well, Jean, I don't approve of tattling, anyway. If Annette were to come to me with some story, you know I would tell her to mind her own business," Mom said.

"What if it were something I really did do and forgot about?"

"I would ask you about it. But do you think I would believe Annette more than I would you?" Mom asked. She set down the sheet she was folding. "Do you really, Jean?"

"I don't know. I never thought about it."

She leaned across the corner of the dryer and kissed me where I was, on the little step ladder. "You shouldn't let anybody make you afraid of your father or me, Jean."

Just then Penny came in with the mail. "Mail call," she announced. "Here's one for me from Jack. Here's one for you and Dad from Jack. Here's the phone bill. Here's one from Aunt Bessie and Uncle Rufus. That's all."

"Oh good," Mom said. "News from Aunt Bessie. I had mentioned to them that it might be nice to have a visit this summer—even though Jack's gone up to Canada. My, it's been years since I've seen Bess and Rufus. Do you remember them, Jean?"

"No. Do they live in Pennsylvania like Aunt Irene?"

"No, Alabama. Uncle Rufus used to raise horses when things were better."

Penny turned around quickly. "Horses? For racing, Mom?"

Mom was startled. "Of course not." Then she laughed. "He got contracts from the marines, sometimes, for parade horses, and from some of the police forces around the country. In cities like Philadelphia some of the policemen are mounted."

"Really?" I asked. "Like real Mounties?"

"Yes, except they wear regular police uniforms and helmets, I think. Being on a horse helps them with crowd control and gives them a good height to be looking from."

"But Uncle Rufus doesn't raise the horses anymore?" I asked.

"Well, not many. Not nearly as many as he used to. Most of the buyers get their horses from Kentucky. Uncle Rufus has just gradually been pushed out of the market, I suppose. He still has his land from when things were going well, and he keeps some cows. And Aunt Bessie is very good at hand crafts—quilts and those things. She always had a taste for it as a girl. So between them both they manage to keep the farm." She set the letters on the dryer. "I'll get to these as soon as I finish this load. It will give me a rest."

"Can we go up to the quick mart for ice cream, Mom?" Penny asked.

The three little kids were at a birthday party. "All right," Mom said. "Pick up some bread, too, while you're there, please."

"Sure. Come on, Jean."

One nice thing about Jack's being gone was that Penny did more things with me. And since Annette was a little scared of Penny—who's not scared of anything—I knew

I wouldn't be running into Annette any time soon. I decided to tell Penny about everything as we walked up to get our ice cream cones.

Every time Annette starts anything about my being adopted, Penny gets really mad. One thing about Penny— she's all for the family. So after I had told her everything I'd been thinking since Sunday morning, Penny said, "I wish you wouldn't let people push you around so much, Jean! That's your trouble!"

"I don't think I let people push me around."

"Oh yes, you do, and don't bother arguing about it. You let people push you around and that's that."

I still didn't think so, but I didn't bother arguing.

"I think Mrs. Bennett's right. What you need is a good dose of danger. Something to make you brave. Like Indian kids."

"Like Indian kids?"

"Sure. They'd go sit on top of a mountain for three days without any food, and when they came back, they'd be brave."

"I think I would be dead."

"No, you wouldn't. You'd learn to go into the woods and fight for your food."

"Most likely I'd get fought over as food." Penny and I both know that I'm scared of most animals. I don't like dogs, and I've never been on a horse, not even those 25-cents-a-ride ponies they have at carnivals.

She looked at me, almost in disgust. "Jean, you are so meek!"

"I can't help it; I was born that way, and you don't make it any better getting mad at me."

She started walking again. "You're right. But I'll tell you one thing, if we get to go down to see Uncle Rufus and Aunt Bessie, we're going to go find a mountain somewhere and make you brave."

"What are you going to do, tie me to it for three days?"

"No. Mom and Dad would get mad. But you're so scared of animals anyway, if we went down to Aunt Bessie's, just having to walk around that farm with its horses and cows would probably make you brave."

I decided that this was *not* the time to tell Penny about my prayer for an adventure. I was pretty sure she'd take it on herself to help the Lord answer it.

Chapter Three
Speaking Up for Myself

A few weeks ago, Mom had asked Aunt Bessie and Uncle Rufus to come up to Peabody for a visit, but they couldn't leave their farm. I wondered if maybe they would invite us down.

Aunt Bessie, I knew, was Mom's older sister. I couldn't remember ever meeting her, but Mom said we had all gotten together when I was really young. Penny told me that Aunt Bessie and Uncle Rufus lived in Scotsville, Alabama. I wondered if they would really invite all of us to come and if we would end up going. It seemed like a long way. Penny said it was about 800 miles. I'd never traveled 800 miles before, not all at once. But when I thought about it, it wasn't as far as Jack and Scruggs were going on their way up to the Yukon.

Just as Penny and I were coming back from the quick mart, I saw Annette waiting for us out in front of our house.

"Now listen, Jean," Penny said quickly, in a low voice. "Don't you get bullied into anything. You stand up to Annette. I'll help you."

"You don't have to do that, Penny," I told her—very honestly. I kind of thought that Penny might make things worse. Don't get me wrong. Penny's a terrific big sister, until she gets these ideas that it's up to her to improve me.

"Oh, I'll do it all right," Penny said. I think that she doesn't like Annette very much.

As we got closer to the driveway, Annette spoke up—"Jean, where have you been?"

"She's been at the quick mart. Tell her, Jean," Penny commanded.

"I've been at the quick mart," I told Annette.

Annette glanced at Penny with that expression that somebody very important in the seventh grade might give to somebody very important in the eighth grade. She didn't want to be rude to Penny, but she didn't want Penny bossing her around, either.

"Well, I wanted to walk over to the park with you today," she said. "I told you that last night."

"So?" Penny asked. "Jean forgot, that's all. Tell her, Jean."

"I forgot," I said.

"Penny," Annette said, and pursed her lips. "I wish you would mind your own business."

"This is my business. Jean's my sister. My sister!" she repeated loudly, because she doesn't like the way Annette is always talking about adoption.

"Well, so what? Jean's my best friend."

"No, she's not. Tell her, Jean."

I just stood there, feeling awful. This wasn't the way it was supposed to work out.

"Jean, what are you waiting for?" Penny asked. "You don't have to be best friends with anybody if you don't want to."

"You be quiet, Penny Derwood. Jean is too my best friend. Aren't you, Jean?"

"Well," I began.

"You're always bossing her around," Penny argued. "She doesn't even have to tell you whether or not you're her best friend. You don't have to tell her, Jean."

"Jean Derwood, if you don't answer me, I'll never speak to you again—and neither will anyone else!" Annette exclaimed.

"Oh, nobody's afraid of you, Annette. You're nothing but a tattletale, and we all know it."

"How dare you! I'll tell your mother! I'll tell Miss Crumble (Penny's Sunday school teacher)!"

"You can tell the whole world, for all I care," Penny said.

"Jean, are you going to let her talk to me like this?" Annette demanded.

I glanced at Penny and back at Annette. "How can I stop her?" I asked. "But look, Annette—"

"Jean, don't let her scare you!" Penny exclaimed.

"I'm not scared. I just want to—"

"Some friend you turned out to be!" Annette exclaimed.

"Well, it's just that—"

"If you don't like her, you can always go home," Penny blurted.

Annette burst out crying. I was really surprised, and I felt terrible.

"You both hate me," she wailed. "It's not fair! You've both ganged up on me!" She turned away from us and ran up the street crying.

"This is terrible," I said.

Penny just stood there, her eyebrows together and her mouth working. I could tell that she was both really mad and really ashamed of herself at the same time.

"I said this is terrible," I told her. "We shouldn't have made her cry."

"Well, why didn't you speak up, then, if you were on her side?" Penny asked.

"You wouldn't let me say anything."

"That's not true. You said a lot."

"You mean I *didn't* say a lot! This is awful. I don't want to be best friends with Annette, but I didn't want her to start crying! Now what am I going to do?" I went into the house by myself, went up to my room, and had a good cry on my own. That was the worst I had felt since the time I'd mistaken Penny's bread dough for my modeling clay and made a model Aztec city out of it and painted it gold.

I don't know what Penny did after I went up to my room. But a while later my Mom came in.

"What's wrong, Jean?" she asked. "Why are you lying down? Are you sick?"

"No," I told her without rolling over or sitting up.

"Have you been crying?"

"Yes."

"What happened?"

"I was crying because I'm a chicken and a big baby, and everybody pushes me around, and I never know what to do about it until too late."

Then she was quiet for a little bit, and finally she rubbed my back for me and said, "What happened that made you cry?"

So I told her about running into Annette and Penny getting mad right away and how they'd both started arguing with each other over whether I was or wasn't Annette's best friend. I knew I should have told Penny that Annette and I would talk about it alone together, and then I could have mapped it out with Annette about how she couldn't push me around anymore and threaten to tell on me, but we could go on being friends. But instead I just stood there because I didn't want to make Penny mad at me, and I didn't want to make Annette mad at me, and now they were both mad at each other, and each was mad at me anyway.

"Well," Mom said when I'd finished. "I think that today you should go over to Annette's and apologize for making her feel like you were ganging up on her. And then if she'll listen to you, you ought to talk to her like you had planned to originally."

"What about Penny?" I asked.

"Well, I'll talk to Penny. But it's up to you to make things right between you and Annette. And it's up to you to make her understand that you want to be friends but you don't want to feel like she's the boss all the time."

I sat up. "Okay." I had never thought that I could hurt Annette's feelings, I guess. It seemed that if she wanted to be friends with me that bad, then we could be friends— I just didn't want to be bossed around or have somebody threatening to tell on me. Maybe someday we could even be best friends.

Chapter Four
Settling Things

A little later I knocked on Annette's door, but her mother told me she had gone down to the park by herself. So I walked down to the Peabody Recreational Park. It has a nice name, but really it's just a swing set, a sliding board, and an old sun-baked basketball court with faded lines and hoops whose nets have been torn off by time and the weather. All of these are set up along a narrow little creek that flooded once, a few years before in the early spring.

Not many people go to the park in hot weather, not during the daytime, anyway. In the evenings there are always men and boys playing basketball from after dinner until it gets dark.

When I got down to the park, Annette was sitting on one of the swings, just looking over at the creek. I could tell she was furious.

"Annette," I said, coming up behind her. She glanced quickly over at me, as if she wasn't sure whether to be mad or to be glad, but then she tossed her head and looked away again.

"Well, what do you want?"

"To say that I'm sorry. And to tell you I didn't mean to gang up on you."

"Sure. You let Penny talk you into anything."

"Well, maybe so, but I'm sorry."

"Well, that's okay, because *I* don't want to be best friends with you anymore."

"Okay."

I just stood there, trying to figure out how to explain that I still would like to be friends somehow with her. But then she got mad at me again.

"So you really didn't want to be best friends with me!"

"I thought you didn't want to be best friends either," I told her. "That's what you just said yourself."

"Jean Derwood, just go away; you're the meanest person I know. And you just wait. Now you think you're big stuff because you get to help Mrs. Bennett on Sundays."

"I do not."

"You just wait, Jean Derwood. You'll be sorry."

There wasn't anything else to say, not if I couldn't get her to listen to me. And I wasn't afraid anymore of her telling on me. So I just said, "Okay, then, I'll wait." And I turned around to walk away.

"Where are you going?"

"Home."

"You hate me, don't you?"

"No, I don't. I just don't like it when you boss me around. We always do what you want to do all the time, and you get mad if I make friends with anybody else."

Annette finally looked at me—really shocked. I guess nobody had ever said anything like that to her.

"So that's what you think!" she exclaimed.

"That's why I said it," I told her. My stomach was shaking on the inside. I felt almost the same as I had felt when she had started crying. It was terrible to get somebody so angry. Then I wondered if maybe Annette only knew how to get along with people by bossing them around. Maybe she'd never even thought about doing things differently. "We could still be friends," I blurted.

"You just don't want to be best friends with me."

"I don't want to be best friends with anybody," I told her, honestly enough. "But I want to be friends with a lot of people. Not just one person."

She looked at me for a minute, and I thought maybe she would give in or maybe even start crying again because her face looked like she might for a second or two. But then she said, "Hmf!" and turned back around to look at the creek. So I stood there like a bump on a log for a couple seconds and then finally turned and walked away.

She didn't bother saying that she would tell on me or anything, because I guess that all of a sudden she realized it wasn't going to work any more. In one instant I realized how silly that kind of threat was and how unlikely it was that Annette would ever really try to carry it out. All of a sudden I knew I'd never have to worry about that kind of thing again. I wasn't afraid of it anymore.

On my way home I felt bad about Annette, but I wondered if maybe this was the way a person grows up. I'd never done anything like facing Annette and telling her the entire way I felt about something. I don't know if I'd ever told a person the whole entire way I felt about anything before. The first thing I would do, I decided, would be to tell Mom all about it.

But when I got home, the first person who met me was Penny.

"Hi," she said, very soberly.

"Hi."

"Did you go to see Annette?"

"Yes, she's at the park."

"Is she still mad at you?"

"Yes." I glanced at her. "Are you going to go talk to her?" I asked.

"Well, Mom said I should. She said I shouldn't have called Annette a tattletale."

"She probably won't be one anymore, anyway," I added.

Penny glanced at me with curiosity, but then she said, "Well, I'm sorry if I got you into trouble with Annette. I just meant to help, but then I got mad."

I shrugged. "That's okay. I mean, it worked out. It kind of helped force me to say what I had to say, I guess."

Penny nodded and walked past to go out the door. "By the way," she said as she left. "Aunt Bessie wrote and said we could all go down to the farm if we wanted. See you." And she left.

I leaned out the door and called after her, "What about the mountains? Are there mountains there?" But she was already too far away to hear what I was saying. Well, it didn't matter about mountains anyway; I was plenty nervous about horses and dogs and getting chased by chickens and geese if Uncle Rufus had any of them running around loose.

With a sigh I walked through the kitchen to find Mom. Somehow I had the idea that all of this was happening to make me a brave person. I hadn't realized what I was getting into when I'd prayed that prayer. But then again, it had felt good not to be afraid of Annette anymore. It could all be worth it.

Chapter Five
News

That night at dinner Mom and Dad talked about the trip down to Alabama. That was when they mentioned that Aunt Bessie and Uncle Rufus had said that one of us older three kids could *stay* for a month on the farm to help out. I guess that he and Aunt Bessie had been thinking mostly of Jack when they'd made the offer, but of course that was impossible now.

"What do you and Penny think about it?" Dad asked. "Would either of you like to spend a month on his farm?"

I sure didn't want to, but just then Mom said, "Well, Jean is a little young to be away from home for so long."

It's funny how sometimes a person can change your whole mind just by agreeing with you on something. As soon as Mom said that, I felt like she was trying to take care of her poor, scared daughter. I wondered if everybody who knew me knew how afraid I was of everything.

I sat there thinking about this while Penny and Dad were talking about farms and horses, and I guess I interrupted without meaning to, but I spoke up and said, "I'd like to do it, Dad."

He and Penny stopped talking and just looked at me, surprised, and Mom said, "Jean, are you sure? A month might seem like a long time."

"I know," I said. "But—I'd like—I'd like to at least try."

Even I hadn't realized how mad I was at myself for being so afraid of everything, but when I said that, my eyes filled up with tears. I wished that everybody didn't just assume that I *wanted* to be afraid for the rest of my life.

Dad looked at me, a little puzzled, but very kindly. "If you want to try, Jean, then we'll leave it up to your aunt and uncle to decide," he said. "They need someone to help them on the farm, and they would ask both of you to stay if they knew that you both wanted to, but your mother and I don't think that would be fair to them— not with the struggle they're having right now. When we go down there, you'll both just have to make yourselves useful and then decide if you really do want to stay down there for a whole month, after all. And if you both still do, then Aunt Bessie and Uncle Rufus will take on whichever one of you can be of the most help."

We were all silent for a minute, even Freddy and Marie and Renee. Then Penny said, "Well, I did get to go to Pennsylvania and San Francisco. Maybe it's Jean's turn."

"That's true," Dad said to her, but he glanced at Mom when he spoke.

"Well, maybe we should wait until we get all the way down there," Mom said. "One of you may decide that a month that far from civilization wouldn't be that much fun anyway."

Dad nodded, and so did Penny and I. But I could tell that Mom thought I'd get too homesick once I got down there. As for me, I thought I might, and I thought

I might get scared of the horses and anything else Uncle Rufus had, but I also thought the whole thing might be the adventure I had asked for in my prayers. If it was, I wanted to go through with it.

After dinner when Penny was tying on her apron, I said, "I'll do the dishes by myself, Penny."

She glanced at me. "You want me to clear the table?"

"No, I'll do it all," I said.

"How come?" she asked.

I shrugged. "I don't know. I just thought I would." Really it was because I was so glad that she had offered to let me stay at the farm, but I didn't know how to say it. But then I looked at her and admitted it: "I guess it's because I'm glad you wanted to let me stay at Aunt Bessie and Uncle Rufus's." I twisted the dish towel up in my hands after I said it, and when she didn't answer right away, I added, "Thanks."

She took off her apron. "You're a good kid, Jean; you know that?"

I smiled. "Thanks."

It was a nice evening—nice and cool. I didn't mind doing the dishes and looking out the kitchen window at the trees on either side of the driveway and the quiet street outside. It felt homey. The sky was pale whitish blue with a few pink streaks just starting across it.

When the kitchen was all tidy, I hung up my apron and dishtowel. I could hear Mom upstairs with the three younger ones, telling them one of their Bible stories.

Penny and I shared a room. I went inside to find a book, and she was sitting on her bed reading; so I flopped down on mine to read. But pretty soon she started asking me about who I wanted to get as a teacher when school started in September, and so we talked about teachers she'd had and teachers I'd had, and then we talked about field trips we'd gone on and filmstrips we'd seen in school. Then we got to talking about trying out for field hockey when we got into high school.

The whole time we were sitting up and talking, it was getting dimmer and dimmer outside as the sun set, and the room got pretty dark, but we could see enough with the light thrown through the window from the streetlight below. I'd never sat and had a long talk with Penny before— unless it was when she was telling me about something that she and Jack had done, but this was different. She wasn't just talking to me—we were talking to each other.

After a long time Mom came in, a little surprised because we hadn't even changed into our nightclothes.

"My, girls, it's eleven o'clock," she said.

We both sat up straighter, surprised. "Eleven o'clock!" Penny exclaimed.

"We talked that long?" I asked.

"Is that what you two have been doing? Well! You must have had a lot of catching up to do. But you'd better get to bed now. Good night."

We changed and went to bed. We did talk for a little while longer, but eventually it was more in just little bits with long, drowsy silences between. But right before I went to sleep, I thought about what a nice sister Penny was and how glad I was to be in my family, even if I was so different.

Chapter Six
Alabama

We left one morning while it was still dim outside. There were a few stars still out. Mom and Dad put blankets in the back of the station wagon, and Freddy, Renee, and Marie—still in their pajamas—climbed in there with their pillows. They were still yawning and stumbling around, and before we even pulled out of the driveway, they were asleep again.

Penny and I sat in the middle seat of the station wagon. We were both yawning, too, and I was chilly. Mom, armed with Thermoses and a big bag full of a box of doughnuts, a box of corn flakes, and a tin of crackers, crowded all her stuff into the front seat. Dad made sure everything was locked and that the oven and stove had been turned off. Then we prayed together and pulled out.

For a long time while the sun was coming up, there was nothing interesting outside the window—nothing unusual, I mean. Then we switched interstates from Route 51 to I-90, and Dad said to start watching for signs for Chicago. Mom passed back doughnuts and milk.

"Are there mountains where Uncle Rufus lives?" I asked.

Dad nodded. "Caves, too."

"Big caves?" Penny asked. "Like Mammoth Cave?"

"I don't know if any are that big," he told us, "but they're big enough to walk through. Your Uncle Rufus took me through one years and years ago when I was in Alabama on a business trip."

Mom shuddered. "They're full of bats—ugh!"

Dad grinned at her and said wryly, "It only takes a few winged mice to ruin that sense of mystery and awe, eh?"

"Not for me!" Penny said bravely.

Dad glanced into the rear-view mirror to smile at her. "Well, you might cool your courage once you get into a real cave, Pen," he said. "I was surprised at how I was affected when I walked into one."

"Why's that, Dad?" I asked him.

"Well, I guess the darkness was a lot darker than anything I was used to," he told me. "It's pretty solid, and you realize very quickly that your safety really hangs on whatever lights you've brought. I was amazed at how poorly the light from my hardhat illuminated the passage where we were walking. Your uncle had brought a coal miner's lantern, and that made a big difference. And again, it gets pretty confusing, even in a simple cave. We came out to a big chamber and had to hunt around the edges for a long time before we found another passageway, and when we found it, it was no higher than above my knee. I had passed it twice, just thinking it was a little niche in the rock. We had to belly our way through for about a hundred feet. I'd never thought I was claustrophobic until then, with a rock wall over my back, a rock wall under my stomach, and a rock wall on either side of me— not to mention Uncle Rufus's feet right in my face. I was glad when the passage widened out and we could crawl again on hands and knees."

"I think it sounds like fun," Penny said.

"It sure sounds interesting," I added. "Did we get caves from the Flood, Dad? Or did God create them?"

"I'm not sure, Jean," he told me. "I did ask your uncle about that while I was there, and he told me that—since nobody was on the scene—we can't be sure about every cave. It's obvious that caves have been deepened ever since creation by the water that runs through them. The water dissolves softer rock and carries it away. So I guess the Flood probably had a lot to do with the making of caves. But since the Lord made the earth complete and mature— with full-grown trees, full-grown animals, and full-grown people—He probably created it with several underground passages, too."

"Did the bats attack you?" Penny asked.

"No. They flew away from us. Some were asleep upside down from the ceiling of the cave, and we looked at one. The bats there are just little bitty guys. When their wings are folded up, they aren't even the size of mice. They just seem a lot bigger when they're on the wing."

I wondered about bears. I'd heard that bears live in caves. "Dad, weren't you worried about bears in the cave?"

He laughed. "To tell you the truth, Jean, I never thought about it at all. I guess one reason was that the cave we went into was pretty close to some houses; so a bear probably wouldn't have used it. And we went into the cave in the early summer, and bears would only use a cave during their hibernation—in winter. Besides all that, I guess that if you didn't meet a bear somewhere near the entrance of the cave, you wouldn't meet one at all. They probably wouldn't like walking around in the pitch darkness any more than I did. And I don't think any bear could have fit into some of the passages we squeezed through."

"Will Uncle Rufus take us into the cave?" Penny asked.

"We could ask him, but I don't know if he'll have enough equipment," Dad told her. "Your uncle was pretty careful to check our gear when we went and to make sure everything was shipshape. He won't take us in unless he has enough hardhats and lights."

"You might just ask him quietly," Mom suggested. "If you're very interested in seeing the cave, he might consent to giving you a private tour."

"That would be a good idea," Dad added. "I don't really want to go a second time, anyway."

Nobody asked me if I wanted to go, too, which was all right because I didn't. From what Dad had said, caves were dark, narrow places where you couldn't get enough light to see by. And I was on Mom's side about the bats. I didn't want any getting in my hair. I couldn't help but give a little sigh and look out the window. If this was the adventure I had prayed for, it didn't seem like it was going to be much fun.

Chapter Seven
A Whole New Place

By midmorning we'd reached the beltway that goes around Chicago. I'd never been to Chicago, and I expected to see a lot of it from the interstate, but Dad said the beltway would go pretty far around the parts I wanted to see. He was right. But we never did seem to get away from the city. It took a long time, and still I could see train trestles below and other big highways, and here and there clouds from factories.

"This must be the biggest city in the world," I said at last.

Dad laughed and said, "Chicago, East Chicago, Hammond, and Gary are all lined up next to each other, sweetheart. It's hard to know where one begins and the other ends."

Penny looked up again from the book she was reading. "I've never seen so many trains and railroad tracks in my life," she said. "Every time I look up, I see some more."

"That's industry," Mom said.

The little kids were dozing in the back, bored with the monotony.

"Is it lunch time yet?" Freddy asked.

"Not yet, but we can break out the tide-me-overs."
And Mom passed back doughnuts for everybody.

"We'll stop for lunch once we get into Indiana and
away from these cities," Dad promised.

We did take a break for the little ones to get changed
and for everybody to stretch his legs. For the rest of the
trip, Freddy, Marie, and Renee all took turns sitting in
the front seat, two hours at a time.

Outside of a little town called Valparaiso, we stopped
and had lunch. Penny asked how much longer the trip
would take, and Dad said "Lots," and grinned at her.

Then I dozed for a while, but when I woke up, hours
later, the afternoon was on the wane, and everything was
green. I sat up, startled. Instead of flat land, it was all
rolling hills—and so green! I looked from one side of the
interstate to the other. The sky was full of pink and blue
streamers, and there were horses on some of the hills. Next
to me, Penny was asleep.

"Where are we?" I asked. "Is this Alabama, Dad?"

"Not by a long shot, Jean," he said. "We're in Kentucky."

"It's so beautiful! I thought only postcards ever looked
like this!"

For some reason he and Mom smiled at each other.
Every now and then, up in one of the rolly green fields,
I would see a house—all wood, with a wooden porch.
The boards of the houses were narrow boards. The houses
looked tight and snug and cozy on the hillsides. Dad called
them frame houses.

"Why?"

"Because the walls are made first and then nailed against
the frame," he told me. "Some of these old farm houses
here are probably older than your mother or I, Jean."

"I wish we lived here," I said. "It would be so pretty."

"Maybe to some of these folks, Wisconsin lakes look pretty good," he said. "But I know what you mean. This is some of the prettiest country there is."

I didn't say anything after that. I didn't want to. I just wanted to look at the hills and the horses and the houses. As the sun went down, some of the houses put their lights on, and it was even prettier to see the soft glow as we drove past.

I guess it was the sunset and the hills and how peaceful the horses seemed, but suddenly I hoped that all this was the adventure I had prayed for. I had been so worried that it was, that I hadn't stopped to think it might be pretty or wonderful or better than anything I had ever expected. I sat in the dim car, hugging my knees and looking out the window, trying to drink it all in and hoping that I would have my adventure, when Mom said, "You're being awfully quiet, Jean."

"I was just thinking," I told her.

"About Annette?"

"No. About something I prayed for a few Sundays ago." Mom glanced at me, but when I didn't say anything, neither she nor Dad asked me about it, and I was kind of glad because I wanted this to be between me and the Lord. I had started to wonder if He would answer a prayer that I had prayed. Mrs. Bennett had said it was a good idea for me to have an adventure, and I felt pretty sure that the Lord wanted me to be braver. So I wanted to know if He would answer my prayer for me, or if I had to wait until I was older or better.

I mean it, I told Him silently. *I want to be braver, and I want to be able to thank You for danger like the knights used to. And I want to know how to pray—if I can ask for things. And please, even if I change my mind later and start to back out, if You have an adventure here for me, please push me into it—"*

Just then Penny woke up and asked me about dinner; so I finished. Dad told us to watch for signs for food and fuel. Later, I wondered if I should have asked the Lord to push me into an adventure. What if He did, and I didn't want to go through with it? But then I forced it out of my mind. If all of this was for me to have an adventure, then it would be the best thing in the world—just to think of the Lord doing all this to give me an adventure, even showing me the hills and the horses. No, no, I wouldn't back out. Not yet, anyway.

After dinner, just about everybody went to sleep. I think that even Mom did, and Dad and I talked quietly for a while about the farmers and the frame houses. He told me that the part of the South where we were going was a part of what people called the "Bible Belt" because it was the last region in our country to give up orthodox Christianity. He told me that there were still plenty of churches in the South, and plenty of good ones, too, though not nearly as many as there had once been. Then he told about the first missionaries who came to America and about the Great Awakening, and other revivals, and D.L. Moody and camp meetings and things like that. I'd never known before how much Dad knew about everything.

After a while I started to doze, and then I fell asleep in the dark, rumbling car.

When I woke up again, I had a crick in my neck from sleeping cramped up. There was a light shining from a doorway, and Dad was opening my car door. "We're here, sweetheart." I had kicked off my shoes in the car, and before I put them on, he just picked me up and swung me up onto a wooden porch. I was standing in front of

a two-story, wooden frame house. And the golden light from the kitchen was spilling over me through the doorway.

I was still sleepy and didn't say anything, just stood there, staring at this house; and then an older woman who wore an apron hugged me and said she was glad to see me and I must be little Jean and I was so welcome. And then an older man with a rugged, kind face took my hand in his and hugged me at the same time, and he said, "This here's little Jean, all right. Welcome to the farm, honeybun. We got a little supper set out for y'all, and you jest feel welcome. I'm yore Uncle Rufus."

I was so happy I didn't even know what to say. It was like I had dreamed about this place all my life and had finally come home to it.

Chapter Eight
Right at Home

I never knew it was possible to start right off liking anybody as much as I liked Aunt Bessie and Uncle Rufus. Like most people do, they started by talking to Penny and asking about the adventures she'd had and telling her how they had saved the clippings from the papers that Mom had sent down.

They made a fuss over Freddy and Renee and Marie, and while Aunt Bessie and Mom took them upstairs to "pop them into bed," as Aunt Bessie said, Uncle Rufus looked at me and said, "Well, Jean, I haven't heard much out of you. How d'ya like the place?"

"It's beautiful," I told him. And I meant it. Everything was wood—the cabinets and the table and even the floor; and the kitchen smelled like pine and like sausage and like a fire in the fireplace.

"Jean's been enchanted with the South ever since we got into Kentucky," Dad said.

"Why, natchurly. She's got good taste, is all," he said with a laugh. "Jus' wait 'til tomorrow, and I'll take ya all over the farm."

"Got any horses these days?" Dad asked him.

"Old Sarge, that's all. He'll be the last thing to go on this farm, I reckon."

They were both silent, and I could see that Dad didn't want to say anything else. It was hard to imagine things being bad for Uncle Rufus and Aunt Bessie—they seemed so happy.

After a moment, Uncle Rufus said, "Well, things ain't what they used to be, that's for sure, but then, Bess and I are gettin' older. The Lord knows I don't need to be keepin' up with peppery horses, anymore. And He's provided for us right along—good times and bad. I ain't worried."

I could see he wasn't. He and Dad chatted about oats and hay and the best way to break horses to saddles. Dad mostly let Uncle Rufus talk. It was interesting to hear him and, just listening to him, I could understand maybe why somebody would want to work with horses. They seemed beautiful to me out in a field, but whenever I got up close to one, it always seemed too big and strong and full of its own will that I got scared of it. I wondered if maybe I would change, but I didn't have much hope of it. The thought of being with a horse—without a comforting wall between us—was still scary.

Uncle Rufus and Aunt Bessie had some children—grown now—whom Mom and Dad remembered. Their names were Rudy and Trixi. The three little ones had been trundled away into cots and beds in Rudy's old room, and Penny and I shared Trixi's old double bed. It was the highest bed I had ever seen, and there was a big dent in the middle of it that we both kept rolling into. Finally we put our pillows into the dent, and that kind of leveled things out.

After we had gotten into bed and the light was out (the light was just a plain light bulb on the ceiling with a string hanging down from it right over the bed), I lay looking out the big window in the room. It had sheer curtains, and it faced a field in front of the house. A pale, ghostly kind of light came in through it, along with the noise of crickets and other peepers, and once, from far, far, away, I heard a train's whistle.

"You still want to stay?" Penny asked me.

"Yes," I said. I knew that she wanted to stay, too. She gave a little sigh—I think it was meant to sound annoyed.

"Why?" she asked.

"I don't know—I just do."

"Well, if you get scared of that horse of Uncle Rufus's, he's not going to want you to stay. You'd have to learn to feed it and curry it and muck out its stall, and you can't do any of that if you're afraid of it."

"I know."

"And you still want to stay?"

"Yes, and now I'm tired; so good night."

She didn't say anything else, but I knew she was annoyed with me for still wanting to be the one to stay, even though I had admitted I was afraid of the horse. When I thought about it, I didn't think it was really fair of me, either, to want to stay when I knew I wouldn't be of much good to anybody. But then, who was I to say that I wouldn't be of much good—and who was Penny to say? It was up to Uncle Rufus and Aunt Bessie, and maybe there would be other things I could do—like dishes, or laundry, or weeding a garden or something. It was still too early to say that taking care of one horse was the most important thing to be done for Uncle Rufus.

In the morning there was a noise I'd never heard before—like a hawk from far away, I told myself. Then I realized what it was—a rooster crowing—and I almost laughed at myself for thinking it was a hawk. I sat up in the bed.

The room was still dark, but the rooster out there was crowing away. Penny rolled over the other way and looked at the clock.

"It's only four-thirty, Jean," she said sleepily. "Go back to sleep."

"I thought roosters crowed at sunrise."

"Roosters crow whenever they feel like it. Go back to sleep."

I lay back down, but I kept my eyes wide open until I could see the first streak of pink in the sky. Then I got up quietly, put on my clothes except for my shoes, and tiptoed outside of the room.

Everything in the hallway was dark and silent. The house seemed big and strange and a little scary.

I groped my way to the stairs and went down the steps. Every now and then one of them creaked, but nothing else made a noise.

The downstairs was lighter than the upstairs. I put on my sneakers and went out the front door and onto the porch. From the front of the house I could see a field and the long winding dirt driveway that led down from the road. But from the side of the house I could see our station wagon and Uncle Rufus's pickup truck and his little car, and beyond that a shed, and way beyond that a big, old, gray barn, and fences running up and down the little hills around the barn and the house.

Uncle Rufus's farm was kind of at the bottom of a low, long mountain; so all his land was rolling land, not flat. And if I found a place to stand where I could get a clear view of the horizon, I could see the blue-gray of mountains and valleys around us.

I wanted to go out and explore, but I thought I should ask first, and there didn't seem to be anybody up to ask; so I sat on the wooden porch facing east and watched the sun coming up. It was chilly and dewy that early in the morning, but it was still beautiful, and I didn't want to go inside.

"Well, hello there!"

I looked up, and there was Uncle Rufus, coming towards the house from the barn. He was still a distance away; so I didn't call back to him for fear of waking everybody up. But when he came up to the porch, I said hello to him.

"You're up bright and early," he told me.

"I was too excited to sleep," I said.

"Ohho! You were, were you? Excited about breakfast, maybe?"

"Well, no, not entirely."

"Maybe excited about seein' the farm?"

"I guess that's it."

"Well, you give me a hand luggin' up some milk to the back porch, and then we'll see about takin' a tour of the place."

"Okay."

I helped him carry the big metal cans up to the back porch, and by then I wasn't cold anymore. He glanced at his wristwatch. "Not but 6:35. We got a half hour till breakfast. Come 'long and let's see the place."

He had been up early milking the cows and putting all the cattle out to pasture. He told me he had about thirty head all told, and that he planned to sell them all in the fall, except maybe one that he would keep for beef for himself and Aunt Bessie. He showed me the wallow and the sty where he would have kept a pig if he'd had one. And then on the shady side of the barn, he showed me the hen coops and the wired-in chicken yard. There were hens out scratching, but when they saw him, they came strutting real fast over towards us, and he laughed at them. "Greedy old things," he said. "You wouldn't think I'd fed them not half an hour ago."

There was a big, fenced-in field that started at the corner of the barn and fanned out. We walked up alongside the fence. The cattle were off in the distance. It seemed like we'd walked a long way before we came to another fenced field. A little double-rutted path ran between the two fences. We started down that path, and then Uncle Rufus whistled between his teeth.

I hadn't really looked around the second field, but then I saw a dark brown horse with a black mane and black legs come trotting down the hill towards us.

"This here's Sarge," Uncle Rufus said. "He's retired from the police force, and I bought him back. He's one of my oldest friends."

The horse made a noise at Uncle Rufus. It sounded high-pitched and irritated to me, but Uncle Rufus said that it was just a nicker, and that it was Sarge's way of saying good morning. The horse leaned over the fence and pushed his head against Uncle Rufus's chest. "He wants an apple, I see," Uncle Rufus told me. He didn't mind the horse at all. "I don't have one just yet, Sarge, but I'll bring you one, by and by," he said. "Say howdy-do to the little lady." And he pushed Sarge's head over to take a look at me. The horse nickered again, and I still didn't think it sounded very friendly. Then he pushed his nose against me, and I jumped back.

"Oh, Old Sarge won't hurt you," Uncle Rufus said.

"He's awful big."

"Yep, he is that. But he's a gentle giant. Gentle as they come. Ain't you, boy?" And he slapped the horse's neck and petted it. Sarge took the petting and then trotted away again.

"A good man might somehow be persuaded to turn against his friend," Uncle Rufus observed, "but a good horse won't. And you can take out stock on that horse bein' a good one." He glanced up at the morning sky. "Well, I reckon Aunt Bessie and the others must be up. We'd best get back."

Chapter Nine
Signs of Adventure

Breakfast was a big meal—bacon, waffles, strawberry preserves, maple syrup, crushed pecans, coffee for the grown-ups, tea for Penny and me, and milk for the three little ones. Aunt Bessie's cat stood at the kitchen door and meowed to come in and get her share.

"Lands," Aunt Bessie said after Uncle Rufus had prayed. "We were starting to wonder where Jean had gone off to, and if she wasn't out with you bright and early. Did you take her on a tour first thing, Ruf?"

"Well, she wanted to, and I was willin'. Introduced her to Old Sarge." Uncle Rufus spread a layer of strawberry preserves over his waffle. "He was mighty pleased to meet her. He's a right good horse and likes kids." I took that as a hint that I shouldn't be afraid of him.

"Did you see the dogs, Jean?" Penny asked. "Their names are Blackie and Babe."

"No."

"They was around the other side of the house," Uncle Rufus told me. He glanced at Mom and Dad. "We keep 'em chained up at night, now. So they won't roam away from the house."

"Why, Rufus? Have there been break-ins around here?" Mom asked.

"Well, not many. Just one big one over in Marietta, Georgia. Jewel robbery, it was. Goose-egg beryl was stolen, but the state police and FBI has been around here all summer thinkin' the thieves holed up in some little town like Scotsville. Little out-of-the-way towns is right plentiful in these parts."

"Goose-egg beryl?" Dad asked. "I never heard of it."

"Well, it's called the Winchester Beryl," Uncle Rufus said, "but when a picture of it came out in the paper, it looked so much like a goose egg that folks 'round here started calling it that. It annoyed the reporters and agents so much that it stuck."

Aunt Bessie laughed. "Yes, they do take themselves so seriously, don't they? They were a little irritated to find out that Scotsville has only one boarding house and that most other folks didn't want paying guests. I suppose that when those reporters came into town, they expected all of us to drop everything and be all caught up with them and their scandal."

"Folks weren't?" Dad asked.

Aunt Bessie got up to put some more waffles on. "Oh, some were, of course. But it was planting time; so folks couldn't drop everything to tag along after every pack of newcomers that came into town. And besides, the papers say that the Goose-egg beryl has had almost as many people killed over it as the Hope Diamond. I reckon most of us thought that maybe it would be a good thing for it to disappear. Such things are more of a curse than anything else."

"Folks' greed is the curse," Uncle Rufus commented. "Well, anyway, most of the reporters cooled their heels here for a few weeks and then left town again. We still got a few around. A couple of 'em went explorin' in Limestone Cave, lookin' for signs that maybe the thieves cached it somewhere in the rocks, but that theory didn't come to nothing."

"Still, one of them wrote a nice human interest story on the cave," Aunt Bessie put in. "We saved the pictures of it that they ran."

Uncle Rufus nodded. "Since then, it's been pretty quiet. But the FBI agents and state police told us all to be careful. Some gas station attendant got himself shot when the thieves pulled into his place, and he figured out who they was. He gave 'em their gas and then called the police— only the crooks figured out what he was plannin' to do; so they circled around and came back just as he was on the phone. That was the end of him. 'Parently those boys won't let anyone get in their way. We decided to keep Blackie and Babe close to the house at night—just in case."

"Well," Dad said after a long pause, "more than likely those thieves are hundreds of miles away by now."

"Yup, more than likely," Uncle Rufus agreed.

Chapter Ten
The Perfect Place for Adventure

Penny offered to help with the breakfast dishes—
something I hadn't even thought of—and Uncle Rufus was
going to take the three little ones out for a ride in his
pickup truck, with Mom and Dad going along to make
sure that nobody got jolted out of the back; so that left
me pretty much to myself.

I went out to the back porch to glance at the dogs,
and they were big dogs, both of them jet black from head
to tail, with brown underneath on their stomachs. I was
glad to see they were still chained. They glanced at me,
and the bigger one thumped his whiplike tail against the
boards of the porch, but I didn't want to get any closer
to them.

Then I walked down toward the barn, and I thought
about everything Mrs. Bennett had told me, and I thought
about being brave, and I thought about whether or not
the Lord was going to have me stay here for a month.
I sure wanted to stay. Somehow from thinking about all
of it, I just went into praying about it.

There wasn't a single good reason I could think of
to stay. Penny could do anything that I could do, only
better. After all, she was older. And Penny wasn't afraid

of the dogs, and she wouldn't be afraid of Sarge. Penny wasn't afraid of anything. Uncle Rufus could take her into the cave, and they would have a good time exploring it. And Penny would always be funny and cheerful and think of things to say and do.

So it wasn't fair to tell the Lord that I *ought* to stay because I was better suited to. But when I thought about everything that had happened since I had prayed for an adventure, and when I thought that Mrs. Bennett was praying, too, then I thought that maybe I should keep asking the Lord to let me stay. And besides, I loved it here. Penny can love any new place and any new thing, but I loved this place because it was this place.

After that I didn't think much about anything, just about how fresh the grass smelled and how beautiful the morning was. I was up by the field where Sarge was grazing, and instead of cutting down the path that Uncle Rufus and I had taken earlier to get back to the house, I kept going up the hill. Sarge was way over on the other side of the field, nibbling at grass.

The climb became steeper, but I kept going up, and finally when I got to the top, I saw that the other side of the hill was more abrupt in its drop—a great slope for rolling down or for sledding down in the winter— if you had the nerve, which I didn't. Then at the bottom of the hill I was standing on, there was a stretch of trees and shrubs like a wide ribbon, and another, higher hill began, only it was so long and rangy and high that I could see it more deserved to be called a mountain. The hill I was on was facing a ridge of that mountain, but the ridge got higher as it ran away from me. It wasn't high like a mountain in Colorado might be high, but it was high enough. If the sun had been in the right position, the mountain across from me would have thrown its shadow over me.

Down at the bottom of it, there was a house. It wasn't like any house I had ever seen before. For one thing, there wasn't any paint on it at all. It was pure weathered gray. For another, it had gables on it, like four high towers—one at each corner. The roofing material was partly blown away so that I could see rafters underneath, but what was left was dark clapboard. It had old shutters and a porch that was sagging only on one end. And most of the windows were boarded up on the inside, but still, they looked like great, sightless eyes staring out at the hilly landscape.

The sight of the house sent a shudder through me. There was something *dead* about it—something unfamiliar and cold and even sinister.

I didn't want to admit it to myself, but it looked like the perfect place for an adventure—the kind of adventure that would make a person pretty brave. I wondered if I should go down and poke around it a little bit. The idea of going into it was still unthinkable, and even the thought of standing on the porch in front of the great doorway was a little too much to bear, but I could test myself to see how close I could get to it.

The ground in front of me was unfenced grass, but on either side of that downhill stretch of grass there were shrubs and trees. I had stood so long looking at the great old house down below that I hadn't been paying much attention to what was going on around me.

For several seconds there had been a rustling and snapping coming up towards me through the shrubs and trees off to my right before I really noticed it.

When I did, I began to wonder about wild animals, and then I thought about *jewel thieves*. I started to edge away back down the path I had come up, when suddenly

a boy appeared out of the trees and underbrush. He was still about twenty yards downhill from me on the steep side, but he looked right at me with a frown, and I knew I couldn't act like I hadn't seen him. And I knew that if I ran away he could catch up with me, because he looked like he was older, and he looked pretty strong and fast.

He came walking right up towards me, and I'd never seen anybody with such a serious face. He had jet black hair and black eyebrows, and they were drawn together in a frown. And he had black eyes, too, but his skin was fair.

"Who are you?" he said when he was close enough.

I hesitated, then said, "Jean."

"Well, what are you doing here? This is private property."

I looked down, then looked back at the field where Sarge was, then back down the hill I had come up from the barn, which was seeming safer and more hospitable every second. The boy was right. It was private property, but it was Uncle Rufus's property, not his.

"This is my uncle's farm," I said.

"Your uncle?"

"Yes."

He frowned more deeply and crossed his arms. "What did you say your name was?"

"Jean."

"Well, that land down there *isn't* your uncle's property." And he pointed down to the big deserted house. Then he looked back at me. "So if you were planning on exploring it, just forget about it." Then he surveyed me from head to foot. "I never heard of Rufus Simpson havin' any kin."

Suddenly I felt angry with him—whoever he was—for acting like I was some kind of criminal just for looking over a hilltop into somebody else's field. He'd really scared me at first, but then I decided that he wouldn't hurt me as long as I was on Uncle Rufus's land. Obviously he knew Uncle Rufus. For a moment I just stood there, a little surprised at feeling so mad, and just getting madder and madder at him for scaring me and cross-examining me like I was some kind of jewel thief myself.

"I said I never heard of Rufus Simpson havin' any kin," he said again.

"Well, I guess you better get your ears fixed," I blurted at him. "Because I'm his niece, and if I ever catch you trespassing on our farm, I'll sic his dogs at you! You're about the meanest person I've met here!" And then I turned and walked really fast away from him.

"What's got into you?" he called, but I kept going.

Chapter Eleven
Bee in My Bonnet

The boy didn't follow me back down the hill. I rushed past the fields and past the barn and then came into the house. Aunt Bessie was at the table, peeling apples. Freddy and Marie and Renee were in the front room playing a game.

Aunt Bessie greeted me with "Uncle Rufus just took Penny out to see Sarge. You could catch up with them if you wanted to."

"No, thank you, Aunt Bessie. Can I help you peel apples? I don't know how, but I can try," I said.

"Sure, honey. Sit down." I sat at the table and she reached back into another drawer for a paring knife. She showed me how to do it, but I wasn't very good. She could peel apples in one long curl, but all I could do was whittle away on one and get the skin off in little chips. Still, she said it was pretty good for a beginner.

After I'd whittled away on the apple for a few minutes, she said, "You came in here lookin' like you had a bee in your bonnet, Jean."

I glanced up at her, then looked back at the apple, which was turning brown where I had peeled it.

"I met a boy up on the hill who scared me."

"Up on the hill above the barn?" she asked.

"Yes ma'am."

"What did he say?"

"He wanted to know if I knew I was on private property, and then he acted like he didn't believe I was your niece. He seemed mad, but then I got mad at him."

"Must have been one of the Maclaran boys. Did he have dark eyes or blue eyes?"

"Dark, I think."

"The older one. He is a serious boy, isn't he? His younger brother Robbie is all jokes and high jinks."

"I didn't like him. I told him if he ever came on the property I'd sic one of the dogs on him." I glanced up at her. "I'm sorry. He just made me mad."

She worked thoughtfully on an apple, got the peel off in one long curl, and then said, "Well, he knows for himself that neither Blackie nor Babe would harm a hair of his head if they saw him. He's been around them too much. But he is an abrupt kind of boy. He needs to know when he's being rude to people." She glanced up at me. "Try not to think too roughly of him. He means well. He's got some things on his mind and a few things stickin' in his craw. But he's a good boy. He'll grow out of that frown he always wears."

We worked in silence for a while until the apples were finished. Then Aunt Bessie mixed them up with cinnamon and butter and sugar. Next she mixed together flour and shortening and rolled out two pie crusts. She dropped each crust into a pie pan, filled the pans with the sliced apple mixture, and then rolled out two more crusts. I helped her trim the edges and seal them. She used a fork to make a pretty design on top of each one and then put them into the oven. Then I helped her clean up.

After that, it was time to get lunch. I set the table, and she rummaged around, bringing out sliced turkey, salami, bologna, Swiss cheese, and American cheese. She led me into a back room that she called her pantry and brought down a big glass jar full of pickles. Whenever Mom made pickles, she always made sweet pickles, which I don't like, but Aunt Bessie's were kosher dill.

Finally she told me that I could go out on the porch and ring the triangle.

I had noticed the metal triangle hanging outside the kitchen door, and suddenly I knew what it was for. It was just like the metal triangles that cowboys used to have on their chuck wagons. I picked up the metal wand that hung on the wall by it and struck all three sides of the triangle several times.

Just then, bouncing all over his back like a marble on the pavement, Penny flashed by on Sarge. She was laughing and squealing, riding bareback. She had one hand holding onto a kind of halter that the horse was wearing. Uncle Rufus came up from the barn, laughing so hard at the sight of her that he kept slapping his leg. Mom and Dad had been taking a walk together to look at the garden out back, and when Mom saw Penny, her eyes got big, but Dad started laughing too, just like Uncle Rufus.

"She's sure got some fire and pepper in her!" Uncle Rufus called to Dad.

Penny managed to rein in the horse. She awkwardly swung down and Uncle Rufus caught her. He was still laughing. "Penny," he exclaimed, "you're medicine for the soul. I ain't never laughed so hard in a year an' a day! Lands, what a pleasure it is to have you here! This place won't never be the same!"

I hung up the metal wand and went inside.

Chapter Twelve
The Hunting Lodge

The next few days passed pretty quickly, and things were soon established into a kind of routine. Penny helped with breakfast; I helped with lunch. For dinner I set the table, and she did the dishes. Sometimes I got a chance to help Aunt Bessie with baking, and I helped her weed in the garden out back.

She called the seven acres of beans, corn, strawberries, cucumbers, lettuce, tomatoes, and melons a garden, but it was bigger than most back yards I've seen. Down in Alabama all the strawberries are picked way before August, but just about everything else was coming ripe and needed tending. Aunt Bessie showed me how to hoe and weed. It was hot, dirty work most of the time, and I didn't like it, but the only other things to do were things I was scared to do.

Penny fed the chickens (I tried it once, but the rooster chased me), helped with the cows, and had even learned to curry and brush Sarge and check his hooves. Except for the very early mornings, she was almost always with Uncle Rufus.

I still got up at sunrise each day. I would wait on the porch until Uncle Rufus came back from the barn, and then we would walk up the hill and look down at the big deserted house on the next hill. My second day at the farm, he told me the story about the house.

"Fellow named Maclaran owned it. It was one of them ante-bellum mansions, you know—real old—built before the Civil War. He had it all stocked with about the best gun collection you ever saw, and all sorts of luxuries. It was his hunting lodge—and he did every kind of huntin' on the land that you ever heard of. He even had fox hunts on it. But his real home was in Atlanta. He just came here for vacations. He'd bring a dozen men up with him and they'd spend a week huntin' and fishin' and then go away again for another three months. He didn't have any children hisself, but he did have two nephews—Angus and Hugh Maclaran. Folks always said that the older, Angus, was no good. His uncle sent him abroad, sent him back to Scotland to see if he'd straighten out when he saw what kind of kin he'd come from over there. The younger brother, Hugh, was educated here in the States. Word had it that Angus was out of favor with his old man and that Maclaran was aimin' to leave everything to Hugh. But when the man died, they couldn't find a will. And all of a sudden Angus come up with a lawyer sayin' he had the will. It left everything to Angus as the older brother.

"Hugh said the will was a forgery, and I guess most folks thought so—Hugh and his uncle bein' so close, and Hugh bein' the steadier of the two boys. I don't understand all the legal gimcracks that the two of them used, but Angus did get all the money and the Scottish property. Hugh put what they call a 'lien' against the lodge here and the American properties. That meant that Angus couldn't do anything with them—nothing that would make any money out of them. So the old house has just stood there, deserted."

"What happened to the two men?" I asked him.

"Angus has disappeared. Most folks think he's in Scotland. Hugh Maclaran owns a little string of hardware stores in the towns around Scotsville. He lives just over that mountain—got two boys."

"Do you think maybe Angus destroyed the real will?"

"I reckon. But just the same, it wouldn't have been like the old man not to have a copy somewhere around. Both he and Hugh knew what a fox Angus was. And I reckon they both knew that if the money got left to Hugh, Angus would try to finagle matters so that he got the money instead."

"But Uncle Rufus, didn't Mr. Maclaran's lawyer know what was in the will?"

"Sure he did, and he testified that Maclaran had left everything to Hugh, but he couldn't produce the will— not the current one anyway, just some old ones. Y'see, a rich man's estate changes; so he has to keep updating his will. Well, the judge reckoned something was fishy because he never would sign the lodge over to Angus, but Hugh never has found the proof needed to get the properties for himself, and so there it sits."

Uncle Rufus ran his fingers through his gray hair. "The two young Maclaran boys have been comin' out to church about a year now, and every now and then their Ma and Pa come out, too. I think the older boy's serious about the Lord. He made a profession of faith about a year ago and has followed through. Not sure about the others though." He looked down at me and smiled. "See, most folks 'round here go to church no matter what they believe. And they can talk the language, if you know what I mean. So you have to wait and see if they mean all they say. Well, it must be 'bout breakfast time. We ought to get down to the house."

I liked talking with Uncle Rufus and listening to everything he had to tell me. I liked the quiet late mornings with Aunt Bessie. I loved the farm and the hills, and I liked watching Sarge out in his field, but I knew I wasn't doing as well as Penny at helping out. I knew I wasn't as interesting and funny as she was.

One by one the days passed by, until there was only one day left, and then the family would go back to Peabody. On that morning before, Dad called Penny into the kitchen and told her that he wanted to talk to her for a minute. Then he told me not to go too far away.

The three little kids were out in the side yard playing. I sat in the quiet front room and waited. But I knew that they would be telling Penny that they wanted her to stay. Probably nobody even knew how much I wanted to stay. Mom was probably sure that I would be too homesick to stay here for a solid month, and Uncle Rufus knew that I was afraid of Sarge. Penny was just the natural choice.

I guess maybe I was feeling sorry for myself, and maybe I was just mad at myself for being so cowardly and quiet and such a milksop, but I cried while I was sitting in the living room. It seemed like I was always getting in my own way whenever I wanted to do something or be something. Probably even the Lord knew I was too scared of everything to have an adventure.

But then I made myself stop crying. The only way to take bad news is to take it like a good sport. Everybody would feel terrible if I cried when they told me that Penny was staying. So I stopped crying and waited for what seemed like a long time, and then Penny came out of the kitchen, pretty briskly and with a high step. And then Dad asked me to come into the kitchen.

All the grown-ups were in there, and there were coffee cups on the table. I sat in the only empty chair.

"Jean," Dad said. "You know that I asked you a while ago if you wanted to stay here for a month to help out your Uncle Rufus and Aunt Bessie."

I nodded.

"Do you still want to?"

I told myself that I should have just politely said no and that Penny could do it if she wanted to. But even though it would have been polite, it would have been a lie because I did want to stay. And I would be a good sport about not being able to, but somehow I was going to let them know I wasn't as big a coward as everybody thought. Almost, maybe, but not quite. So I said, "Yes, I'd like to stay."

"All right," Dad said. "Your mother and I have agreed to leave it up to you. You can stay."

For a second I just looked at him blankly. Then I said, "I can?"

"Yes. We explained it to Penny that you wanted to stay pretty badly, and—like she said earlier—she's been to Pennsylvania and San Francisco; so it's your turn now. She agreed and thought it would be for the best, and she's pretty sure you'll have a good time."

"Thanks, Dad." I looked at Uncle Rufus and Aunt Bessie. "Thank you," I said.

"Why, don't thank us!" Uncle Rufus exclaimed. "We're gonna' put you to work!"

But Aunt Bessie smiled. "You never mind him, Jean. You're very welcome."

I stood up to go, and Dad followed me out. "Jean," he said softly. I turned around. "Make sure you thank Penny," he said. "She's been a good sport about it."

I nodded. I knew exactly how Penny felt, and I was glad she was willing to let me stay and act like she didn't mind that much.

Chapter Thirteen
Getting Acquainted

On Saturday morning we all ate breakfast while it was still dark outside. Freddy was so sleepy he put his shirt on backwards. Mom and Dad had packed up the car the night before. There still weren't any lights in the sky when we all went outside into the warm, damp, early morning to say good-bye.

Dad kissed me and said he'd see me in exactly four weeks. Mom made more of a fuss and was sure to tell me I could call once a week—or even more if I thought I had to. And she kept hovering near me until everybody else was in the car. Then she gave me one last kiss and a hug and said to remember to pray for everybody and she would see me soon.

I think, as I saw the car's tail lights going way up the winding driveway into the dimness, that maybe I got a tight spot in my chest. I wondered if I'd made a big mistake. But right away I told myself that anybody can last a month anywhere. And just then Aunt Bessie put her arm around me and hugged me up to her apron, and I believe that was the last time I was homesick.

We went inside and cleaned up the breakfast dishes. By that time the sun was coming up; so I went out with

Uncle Rufus to help in the barn. He took Sarge out and I mucked out the stalls. Then I got the big sack of powdered milk and mixed up warm milk for the calves that had been separated from the herd. Uncle Rufus fed them, not because I was afraid of the calves, but I think he didn't want me to make pets out of them. They were going to be sold soon.

Uncle Rufus then showed me how to feed the chickens. I was still afraid of the big rooster, but he showed me how to flip half a handful of feed sideways. The rest of the chickens missed it, and the rooster always ran after it instead of chasing the person who had come into the yard. Then I realized that the rooster had probably started chasing people when he realized they would flip him that little half-handful to keep him quiet.

"He's a smart one," Uncle Rufus told me, "but he's going to end up in the soup one of these days." I didn't feel sorry for the rooster.

Uncle Rufus wanted to work on his tractor, and he said I could help him; so I spent most of the morning talking with him and handing him his tools while he climbed all over the big, high engine of the tractor.

Later we drove out in the pickup truck, and he showed me the two other fields he had. One of them was alfalfa. He told me he'd once used up all his own alfalfa feeding his horses, but with times being so bad, he sold most of it as feed. The chaff that was too dusty for horses he used as cattle feed.

The other field was just empty, with a light covering of straw and old stems and roots. He said it was resting, but he would plant it the next year.

While we were out in the truck, he said he would show me the cave entrance. I was glad we didn't have any caving gear with us because I still didn't want to go into it to explore.

He pulled the truck onto the road that ran in front of the farm, and we followed it past the farm and around the bottom of the ridge where the deserted house was, and then up the steeper part of that mountain. The road twisted and turned around the side of the mountain as it wound its way up. Then Uncle Rufus abruptly turned off the highway and up a little double-rutted trail. The truck jounced and bounced over big loose rocks and deep ruts. He pulled to a stop, and we climbed out.

I guess I had always imagined the mouth of a cave being surrounded with awe and mystery, so that if a person ever drove by one, he would automatically feel his eyes attracted to it, like a compass needle to the north. But I just stood there looking around, waiting for Uncle Rufus to lead me to the cave, until he laughed and said, "Don't you see it?"

I glanced at him, then followed his gaze, and sure enough, there it was. It was big, too, plenty high enough for me, though Uncle Rufus had to stoop just a little bit in the entrance.

I couldn't see into it at all. It was as though a wall of darkness began just a foot or two inside the entrance. There didn't seem to be any gradual dimming until darkness. Unexpectedly, a cold breeze blew softly from the interior. I glanced up at him.

"It's called a blowing cave," he told me. "Feel that wind? No matter how hot or how cold it gets out here, it's always about fifty degrees in there, with a light breeze."

"It's so dark," I said.

"As dark as the inside of the earth, Jean. Once you get past the entrance passage, there ain't no way for light to get into it."

A bird flew past, right into the cave, and I glanced at it as it darted by. "How can it do that without hitting the walls?" I asked.

"Oh, bats was made to see in the dark," he said.

I grabbed his hand. "That was a bat?"

"Sure! You didn't think a bluejay would fly into a cave, did you?" He smiled down at me. "Bats won't hurt you. They got lots of their own business to attend to. That's why they go so fast."

"What kind of business?"

"I don't know. I can't get 'em to slow down enough for me to ask."

Then he smiled again and asked me if someday I would like to go into the cave.

The thought of the cold, absolute darkness sent a shudder through me. I said, "Someday, maybe. I don't know if I could do it yet, not unless it's the adventure I prayed for. Oh, I never told you about that."

He looked curious, and I explained about starting to pray for an adventure weeks ago.

He mused on that a little bit, then said, "Well Jean, courage ain't everything, unless it's the courage to do what's right, and you seem to have that."

"Maybe, but I want the courage to do other things— other things that other kids do without even thinking twice about them! Besides, doesn't it look to you like the Lord has been answering my prayers?"

"Now that's a question worth ponderin'," he said. "Y'know, when we ask the Lord to hear our prayers, we're submitting ourselves to His will in settling the problem at hand."

"You mean you think He won't answer my prayer?"

"Oh, I think He'll answer yore prayer, but maybe not in the way you pictured it. Seems to me you want Him to give you courage, but maybe first He's going to have to show you what it is and what it isn't that you been askin' for."

I didn't understand what he meant by that, and I looked at him, waiting for him to go on, but all he said was, "Remember, Jean, courage ain't a substitute for godliness. Satan mightta' been brave enough to attack the throne of God, but he was still a rebel and a fool and got thrown down from his glory. And we seen it here on earth. Adolf Hitler got himself wounded in World War I, serving his country, but he was still one of the biggest scoundrels the world's ever known."

"Well, I don't want to be wicked, Uncle Rufus. I just want to be a good Christian *and* be brave."

"Okay, Jean. We'll have to see what happens."

After that we climbed back into the truck and went back to the farm. Uncle Rufus told me that I was a real treasure to have. I liked that. I told him I was glad to be at the farm.

Chapter Fourteen
Scotsville and Local Color

I hadn't realized how hungry I was until we got home. Aunt Bessie had lunch ready. Over chicken soup (not the rooster) and sandwiches, she told Uncle Rufus that the people from the hardware store had called to say that a part for the tractor had come in that morning.

"Well, I reckon we'll go pick it up after lunch," he said.

"I suppose you mean you and Jean," she said.

"Sure. You come too," he told her.

"Go on now. I got better things to do than laze around a hardware store. Don't you go spoilin' your niece now, Rufus."

"Oh, I ain't spoilin her, am I, Jean?" he asked me. "We did a whole pile of work this morning, and I got her acquainted with the place. While we're in town, I'll look up some folks to see who's coming to the service tomorrow."

"Well, all right, then. Do as you think best, Rufus Simpson, but we got Molly to answer to at the end of the summer; so don't you go filling her daughter up with ice cream from the Tastee Freeze right away."

"Don't you worry, Bessie."

I offered to help with the dishes like I usually did, and I think Uncle Rufus wanted me not to bother, but he didn't say anything. So I helped Aunt Bessie while he stumped upstairs to change his boots for shoes and find his checkbook. Aunt Bessie had seemed a little stern at the table, but while we were wiping up, she put her arms around me and told me not to mind what she said to Uncle Rufus and to go along and enjoy myself.

"If I didn't tell him what to do every now and then, he'd think I wasn't feeling well," she said chuckling. "But, I declare, it's been so long since we've had kin or children here, it makes a body want to take a vacation."

The trip to town took about twenty-five minutes. First we went into the hardware store—Maclaran's Hardware and Parts, the sign said.

Inside, it smelled clean, and everything from the racks shined and gleamed. There were nuts and bolts and crank handles in one section; garden tools and sickles and shears in another; rows and rows of all kinds of light fixtures, and—in the very back—riding lawn-mower models and lots of bigger equipment.

There were a counter and a cash register back there too. Uncle Rufus stepped up to the counter and rang a small bell. "Hello!" he called.

"Be right there!" a voice called back.

He grinned at me. "I'm going to run and pick up a can of oil," he told me. "You stay here and tell the fellow that Rufus Simpson's come about the part he ordered, okay?"

"Sure," I said. He hurried up the aisle. I glanced at the items around me until I heard someone in boots clumping through the back room and out to the counter. When I turned around, there was the tall, dark-haired boy who had talked to me in such a mean way a few days ago. Of course. He was one of the Maclaran boys.

"My Uncle Rufus came to pick up the part he ordered," I said stiffly. "He's gone to get a can of oil for you to ring up, too."

The boy looked a little embarrassed, but he mumbled something and went into the back to get the part for Uncle Rufus. He came back out with a small paper bag and rang up the total on the old-fashioned cash register. Then we both waited in awkward silence until Uncle Rufus came back. Anyway I could see it was awkward for the boy. I didn't care because I was still mad at him.

Just then another boy—closer to my age—came running down one of the aisles with a doughnut in his hand. He stopped at sight of me. "Hi," he said. He had dark hair, too, and dark, straight eyebrows. He looked enough like the other boy for me to guess that they were brothers, but his eyes were pale blue.

"Hi," I said back.

He paced a little closer, curious, and not at all shy. "Are you new here? You must be staying with someone. I bet it's the Simpsons. Bruce said they had folks staying with them. If you're here for a while, I've got a dirt bike! Two people can go on it at once."

"Robbie!" The older boy, who I guessed was Bruce, spoke sharply. "Mom wanted you to unpack some of the stuff today. Where have you been, and where did you get that doughnut?"

"Where do you think?" he asked. "I bought it up the street." Then he glanced at me. "I'm Robbie Maclaran, and I live pretty close to the Simpsons' farm. Did you know about the giant anthill that's up in the woods about a half mile from your place? I could show it to you."

"Sure." Just then Uncle Rufus came back down one of the aisles, a can of 10W-40 in each hand.

"Hey, Bruce; hey, Robbie," he called to them. He put the cans on the counter. "Ring it up, if you please," he said. "That'll be all for today."

While Bruce rang it up, scowling, Uncle Rufus said, "Have you boys met my niece? She'd likely be a nice change of company for you. Not too many kids around here."

"We met," I said to Uncle Rufus. Then I said to Robbie, the younger Maclaran, "My name's Jean."

He gave a nod and was about to say something when someone behind me distracted his attention. I turned as he ran past me. Even though we were in the back of the store, the building ran lengthwise with the street so that there was still a front window near us. It was cluttered with a row of hanging rakes and shovels, but Robbie crowded in among them. "There he is, y'all! There's the hermit!"

"Would you quit staring, Robbie?" Bruce exclaimed.

Curious, I went to the window too. A middle-aged man was walking past on the sidewalk. His gray hair was long, greasy, and matted. He had a long and dirty gray beard too, ragged clothes, and a shopping bag. He carried the shopping bag in the crook of one arm, and as he walked, he looked neither to the left nor to the right, just straight ahead, with his head a little bowed.

After a brief glance, Uncle Rufus said, "Bruce is right, kids, don't stare so. It ain't polite." I stepped away from the window, and Uncle Rufus turned to Bruce. "Will you be comin' to the service tomorrow?"

"If Dad'll spare me, I'll be there," he said with a nod. Uncle Rufus glanced at Robbie, who shrugged.

After that, we left the store and went into the hot street. We stopped into a shoe repair store, a barber shop, and

a sporting goods store. At each one, Uncle Rufus introduced me to the people in charge and asked if they would be coming to church the next day. Some of them called him Rufus, and some called him the preacher, and I realized that he was the man who ran the services, even though he wasn't a real pastor. He explained it to me when we got into the truck. "See, Scotsville's real tiny, Jean, and there ain't many churches to start with, and what there are ain't preachin' anymore that the Bible's the Word of God. There's a little church building that some Christian fellers and I worked on this past spring. We got it fixed up. I gen'lly do the preachin' on Sundays. Sometimes to a dozen people, sometimes just to Aunt Bessie and maybe one other person."

"What about the men who helped you fix up the building?" I asked him.

"Oh, they was from another church about seventy miles away. I'd been to see their pastor a few times about the condition of the few churches around here. He sent them to help me out with the building, but they're either too young to preach here or have been called somewhere else. And anybody that comes here to preach has to have a steady job doin' something else, because there ain't enough folks to pay a preacher a salary here." He shrugged. "So I fill in. The Lord knows what's best."

Then we went to the Tastee Freeze, and he got me an ice cream cone and one for himself.

Chapter Fifteen
The Maclaran Boys

We drove to the outskirts of town where the deserted railroad tracks sprawled across the road and the fields as if they were asleep. As we drove along past an old, dull green house near the tracks, Uncle Rufus told me that it was where the hermit lived. He'd showed up in town about a year ago and just kept to himself.

"I've invited him to church," Uncle Rufus told me, "But if you talk to him, he just stares right through you and keeps on going. Some folks say he's not right in the head."

That night Aunt Bessie popped popcorn over a low fire in the fireplace. Uncle Rufus told stories a while before he went to finish his sermon. It was hardly eight o'clock before I went to bed. I don't think I'd ever been more tired.

Now I slept in the bed by myself, kind of cradled in the dent in the middle. It was comfortable. I couldn't believe that everybody had left just that morning. It seemed like I had been at the farm for most of my life.

For a while I lay watching the breeze play with the sheer curtains, and then I fell asleep.

Sunday morning we were up at the same time to do the morning chores. Then we all dressed up, and we took the four-door car out instead of the pickup truck. We drove over rolling hills and mountains until Uncle Rufus turned off the quiet highway onto a paved, unmarked road. After about a quarter mile he turned onto a dirt road, came around a bend with a stand of trees, and there was the church—a small white building with a steeple but no bell. There were two cars parked there.

Inside, the church smelled like a hot wooden building—which was exactly what it was. There was no air conditioning, and not enough breeze to make much difference through the open windows. There wasn't any baptistry, either, just five rows of small pews on either side of a narrow aisle, and a plain wooden pulpit in the front.

Aunt Bessie and I sat down. Bruce Maclaran was sitting in the front row, alone, with his usual frown, but at least the frown was more relaxed today. There was an older man and his wife in the front on the other side of the aisle, and across the aisle from us there was the barber and his wife. I guessed that they had brought Bruce with them.

We sang "The Old Rugged Cross" and "Amazing Grace" and had the offering. Then Uncle Rufus preached—just as if the church was full. When he was finished, we stood and sang "Just As I Am," and then church was over. I had never thought about people who had to struggle to keep a church going, but it seemed to make things better to me. Or maybe I liked church here better because I knew how much having the church in Scotsville meant to Uncle Rufus.

After everybody had shaken hands and chatted a little, we got into our cars and went home. In the car we talked about the sermon. That night at seven we went back for the evening service, and this time it was just Aunt Bessie, me, Bruce Maclaran, and the barber and his wife. The other couple wasn't there.

Afterward, Aunt Bessie and Uncle Rufus got to talking pretty seriously with the barber and his wife, whose names were Mr. and Mrs. Handley, about some of the people they had been talking to about the Lord. I was hot inside the still church building; so I went out front. Bruce was already out there. He turned around when I came down the two steps.

I didn't know what he was going to say—I was thinking it wouldn't be very friendly, but then he surprised me.

"Nicer out here, isn't it?"

"Sure is cooler," I agreed.

"I'm sorry I scared you the other day," he said. It was out that easily. He just said it pointblank to me—still frowning in his usual way. But he looked me straight in the eye. And I realized that Bruce just frowned all the time—even when he wasn't feeling bad.

"That's all right. I knew I couldn't sic the dogs on you, anyway. I just said it."

"You come onto our land any time you like, but be careful of the house. It's a trouble spot, and folks other than me would get mighty mad at you for walking around on the place."

"I just like to look at it from the top of the hill," I told him.

Then we were both quiet. I wanted to say something to him because I'd gotten the idea from Uncle Rufus that the only kids around were the Maclaran kids; so if I was going to have any company all summer, it was going to have to be them.

"I guess you and Robbie have been to that cave, too," I said.

"Well, yeah. That's another place to be careful," he told me.

I didn't catch the warning sound in his voice, and I just went on and said, "Maybe someday—later, I mean—we could go in there." I'm not sure why I said it because I really had no desire to go into that cave. I guess I'd been thinking that if the Lord was going to give me an adventure, it would be that cave, and so I'd have to go into it sooner or later.

But Bruce's frown deepened, and he said, "Caves can be dangerous places. You have to be careful in them, especially with you being a girl and so green."

I was so startled to have him call me green that I blushed and said, "Well, sure, I know that." Then I was embarrassed at admitting I was green, or a newcomer. I wondered if this boy had to be down on everything. Just when he started to be friendly, he seemed to change his mind. I sighed and walked away from him, through the fragrant, cool air towards the cars. Maybe he thought girls were silly. Or maybe he thought everybody was silly. Just then Uncle Rufus and Aunt Bessie came out of the building with Mr. and Mrs. Handley. Uncle Rufus locked up the church. As we started climbing into our cars, Bruce came up to me.

"If you want to go into a cave," he said, "let me take you. Robbie's too scatterbrained to do it. Okay?"

"If anybody takes me into the cave, it will be somebody who I have confidence in," I told him sharply. "Probably Uncle Rufus."

He stepped back. "Okay," was all he said. But I think my answer embarrassed him. Maybe he realized again that he'd been rude to me.

"Why does he think he can boss everybody around?" I asked Uncle Rufus when we were driving home.

He glanced back at me. "He is older and knows better, honey-bun. I'd listen to him. He does a man's work during the summer."

"Well, all I said was that I'd like to see the cave someday. And I got a lecture from him. Just like the time I was looking at the big old house. He's so bossy. No wonder Robbie won't listen to him."

"Well, Robbie's another story altogether. That boy's still got some oatmeal between his ears."

"Rufus!" Aunt Bessie exclaimed.

"Sorry," he said, with a sheepish grin at her. "Anyhow, Jean, you can trust Bruce's opinion, even if he does give it too freely. And he does have a lot more sense than Robbie. Don't be rough on him in your heart. He's a new Christian, and he ain't used to getting along with strangers. Everybody around here's known him all his life and has gotten used to him. Just bear with him. I think you'd like to have his friendship."

I nodded and sat back, but privately I thought it would be easier to make friends with a bear than with Bruce Maclaran.

Chapter Sixteen
Sarge

The next morning while we were doing chores, Uncle Rufus talked to me about the courage I'd been praying for.

For some reason I liked thinking about the courage the Lord was going to give me a lot more than I liked talking about it with Uncle Rufus. I got the idea that he had a completely different way of looking at it than I did. I told myself that he must be wrong, because Mrs. Bennett had looked at it the way I did. But I guess I didn't really know that. She and I had only talked about it once, and all she had said was that she was going to pray for me to have an adventure. All the thinking about it and planning things out had come from me.

Anyway, that morning Uncle Rufus started telling me all about Sarge and what a good horse he was and how gentle he was. I knew he was hinting that I ought to get to know Sarge a little better. I didn't know what to say. Sarge was awfully big, and he was just a horse, which meant he wasn't as smart as a person, which meant he might be dumb enough to step on me or bite me or something.

"Listen here, Jean," Uncle Rufus said to me as we walked back to the house. "You got to learn one thing about courage: it's hooked right up with trust. Folks who are brave are either trusting themselves or trusting the Lord or trusting someone else. I think if you'd just trust my judgment about that horse, you'd get near enough to him to trust him, and then you'd get over bein' scared of him. He ain't never hurt a child all his life, and he's just as affectionate and tame as a puppy. He's the best horse I've ever had."

I didn't say anything because I was still scared of Sarge. Then Uncle Rufus gave it up, and I thought from his silence that he might be mad at me.

We went in and ate breakfast, and he was as nice as you please. Then I figured that maybe I had hurt his feelings because I was still so scared of his favorite horse. After breakfast I went out to work in the garden a while, under the watchful eyes of Babe and Blackie. They were tied, and they sat watching me. Every time I came down a row close to them, both their tails would start thumping against the porch floor. Then as I worked away from them, they would quiet down. Then as I came back down the row, their tails would start going again.

After I was finished weeding and hoeing, I filled the dogs' water bowls for them from the spigot outside. Their tails started going again as I set the bowls down. After they had drunk some water, I stepped closer. They flopped down again on the porch, their tongues lolling. I let my hand come closer to Babe to pet her head. She jerked her nose up to sniff my hand, then thrust her head up into my palm. Blackie stood up and came around. I didn't want to move too quickly around them, but I was afraid they might both jump up on me. But all he did was get his head between me and Babe so that I had to pet him instead of her. He flopped down. I'd never known dogs could be jealous like that, but Blackie was. He didn't want Babe getting any petting that he didn't get.

After a few minutes I started petting them both. It was really too hot outside for them to be jumping up, anyway, I thought. After a while I went back into the house.

I helped Aunt Bessie get lunch ready, and soon Uncle Rufus came in. After we had prayed over the food, I said, "I could go up with you to see Sarge this afternoon, Uncle."

He glanced up at me, a little startled, then he smiled at me, and he said, "All right." Then I realized that he hadn't been mad at me that morning, but it had hurt his feelings for me not to trust his judgment and his favorite horse.

I didn't ride Sarge that day. All I did was stand out on the path on the outside of Sarge's pasture. Uncle Rufus went in through the gate and whistled. Sarge came trotting right towards him.

"Now Sarge, I got a little lady for you to meet," Uncle Rufus said. "You've met her before, but not up close." He brought him outside the fence so that there wasn't anything between us. I had thought that Uncle Rufus would lead him up to me by his halter, but then he let Sarge go, saying, "There she is right there. Go up and say how d'ya do."

The horse turned and started coming down the hill toward me—awfully fast, I thought. I shut my eyes as he came. I could hear his hooves, and then, nothing. Just a tickling on my side. I opened my eyes to see him trying to get his lips inside my pocket. He turned to the other pocket and then nosed my trembling hand. He turned and nosed the other.

Walking down the hill toward us, Uncle Rufus laughed. "He thinks you've brought him something," he said. He dug into his own pocket and pulled out a sugar cube. When Sarge was on my other side, Uncle Rufus passed it to me. I really didn't want to feed a cube of sugar to something with teeth as big as Sarge's teeth were.

"Should I hold it flat on my palm?" I asked. But just then Sarge saw it, shot out his tongue and—with a tug of his lips—got it safely from my hand into his mouth. I blinked.

"Go on and pet him," Uncle Rufus said.

I lifted my hand and patted Sarge on the bridge of his nose. He pushed against me with his nose and sputtered with his lips.

"He's right pleased to meet you," Uncle Rufus said. "Ain't you, Sarge?" At Uncle Rufus's voice, Sarge turned to him, and I watched Uncle Rufus pet him and slap his neck with the familiarity and expertise of a real horseman. After a while he put Sarge back in the pasture. "Now," he told me, "you come out here every day, and pretty soon you'll get to know each other right well. Wouldn't be surprised if by the end of the week you was ridin' him."

When Uncle Rufus said that, I thought I'd never get brave enough to get on that high back. But really, as I saw Sarge day after day, without a fence between us, I got less and less scared of being on his back. For one thing, he was kind of old—not so old that he couldn't take a rider, but too old to do any jumping around or fighting back against a rider. For another, he seemed to know I wasn't as big or as old as Uncle Rufus.

The next Saturday when Uncle Rufus showed up with an old Western-style saddle, I was willing to try riding Sarge.

Uncle Rufus showed me how to use the reins and how to keep them relaxed and how to try to grip with my knees. I rode a little bit in the morning under Uncle Rufus's watchful eye. But in the afternoon I felt so good about it that he just saddled Sarge up and told me not to go too far away but to have a nice time. The horse and I rode off up the hill.

Since Bruce had told me I could go on their property, I rode Sarge along the top of the hill until I found a less steep way down onto the Maclaran land. We struck a little path that wound along in the tall grass and then dropped into the shrubs and trees. Sarge seemed to like it. We jogged along for several minutes. Most of that time we were hidden from sight from either the top of the hill or the big old house, but when we finally broke out of the cover, I realized that we'd come down pretty far. As we came around a stand of trees, I found myself staring right at the front of the house.

It didn't spook the horse, but it sure spooked me. I was a lot closer, and it was a lot more forbidding than I had thought. We were only about twenty yards from the front doorway. I started to turn him around and get out of there, when suddenly I heard something—something from the back of the house. Was it Bruce, I wondered. If he saw me getting out of there really fast, he might think I was up to something.

Without really wanting to, I turned and looked. A figure came around from the back of the house, stopped, and looked up. I saw matted beard and hair and in the next second recognized the hermit from town.

He looked up and let out a yell of surprise or anger. His cry sent a chill of fear right through me. "Go!" I yelled to Sarge, just as the hermit started for us. "Go, Sarge!"

That good horse must have known how scared I was, because he took off like a shot when I kicked him, and he didn't run like any old horse, either.

I don't know how I stayed on as he took those curves on that path, except that it was like floating to feel all his legs going like that. I must have known more about horse riding than I'd allowed, because I realized at the end that I was crouching forward, watching his head and moving with it. My free hand was clutching the saddle horn.

We topped that hill at a run, but then I pulled back really hard on the reins (probably too hard) and said, "Easy, Sarge, whoa, whoa!" He gradually slowed and came to a trot. I brought him all the way down the hill toward the house. I was all in a tremble, and Sarge was all in a tremble. Maybe the hermit had spooked him, or maybe my own fear had done it.

As we rode up to the house at a trot, Uncle came out. At first he thought we were just riding up to show off, but when he saw me pull Sarge to a stop and got a look at us, he came up and took Sarge's head while I dismounted. Then he caught hold of my arm with his other hand. "What is it, honey-bun? You're both scared."

In as few words as possible, I told him about the house and the hermit. He looked serious. "Go on in," he said after a minute. "I'll take Sarge in and rub him down."

"What about the hermit?" I asked. "What if he comes here?"

"Don't you be scared of him," Uncle Rufus said. "Whatever anger a man might show in a deserted place sheltered by trees, he ain't going to do much in an open place guarded by two big dogs and in full view of the highway. Go in now, and I'll be in presently."

So I went inside.

Chapter Seventeen
Puzzling It Out

After Uncle Rufus got back from the barn, we sat on the front porch, and I told him again everything that had happened.

"Jean, are you sure that he was mad?" Uncle Rufus asked. "Maybe he was just surprised. Perhaps he just wanted to know what you were doing there."

"No, I know he was chasing me—I—" Then it came back to me—*there had been something in his hand!* "He had something," I said. "He swung it up like he might have hit Sarge with it. I barely saw it because I was already turning around to run Sarge away by the time I realized there was something in his hand."

Uncle Rufus looked deadly serious. "Jean, if he did that—are you sure?"

"Yes. I mean, I can't be perfectly sure he would have hit Sarge, because maybe the thing was just in his hand. I mean—it doesn't seem like he'd have any reason to hurt us if he wanted us out of there."

"Did he swing it?" Uncle Rufus asked. He repeated the question, punctuating each word: "Did—he—swing—it?"

"I'm not sure. I barely got a glance at him when he was doing it. It wasn't until after I stopped running that I had a chance to think about it, and then I was mostly scared about seeing his face so shocked when he came around the building. I thought mostly about the way that he yelled—it was so scary. I didn't even think about the pipe in his hand."

"Pipe?"

"I think that's what it was—some kind of metal pipe— straight and black. Maybe it was part of a drainpipe. Or maybe it wasn't. It seemed like it was bent at one end."

Uncle Rufus shook his head. "I'm going to unsnap Babe and Blackie," he told me. "I want you to stay here in the house or on the porch with your Aunt Bessie."

"What will you do?" I asked.

"Talk to Hugh Maclaran about prowlers around the old house. And then we'll go pay a visit to that hermit and get the truth out of him."

I nodded. "Okay."

"And listen here, honey-bun. I don't want you mentionin' it to Robbie or Bruce."

"I won't even see them until Sunday, anyway, Uncle."

"No, they'll be comin' over for a visit tonight. Just the same, don't say anything. If you tell Robbie, it'll be all over town by morning. And if you tell Bruce, it'll just worry him. That boy frets too much over things meant for his elders."

"Okay, I won't say anything."

Just then Aunt Bessie came out. "I finally got Hugh on the phone," she said. "He's going to drive over. He wants to check the house with you before you go into town."

Uncle Rufus nodded. After a moment he said, "Well, let's not be a set of gloomygusses. We'll be havin' comp'ny tonight. Why don't you two throw together a pie or two, and I'll give you the whole story when I get back."

"All right, Rufus Simpson," Aunt Bessie said. She called him by his full name whenever she was worried about anything. I went inside to wash my hands, but before I got out of earshot, I heard Uncle Rufus say, "Ain't a thing to worry about, Bessie, but you got Babe and Blackie here, and the shotgun in the cabinet's loaded. But I'm thinkin' that hermit mighta' cleared outta' town right off if he figured that Jean had caught him red-handed at something."

"Burglary?" she asked.

"That's what I'm thinkin'. But what he expected to find in a deserted hunting lodge—unless maybe he really is out of his head." Then his footsteps went creaking down the porch steps, and Aunt Bessie came inside.

A little later I heard a truck pull up, followed by Uncle Rufus's hearty greeting. After a pause the sound of the truck died away. I looked out the side window and saw Mr. Maclaran's pickup go ambling up the hill toward the ridge and his uncle's lands.

Aunt Bessie called me back to help her, and she kept up a steady prattle of talk and little jokes while we worked stemming strawberries for strawberry pie. I knew she was pretty nervous about burglars, and she wanted me to stay in the kitchen with her. I agreed with Uncle Rufus myself. My imagination wanted to tell me that the hermit was probably hiding somewhere nearby, but if he had been, the dogs would have gone wild. I figured that he was long gone—that maybe he had decided we would call the police on him.

Of course, if I had really had courage like Penny or Jack or most other kids, I would have gone straight back to the old hunting lodge and would have poked around and found a clue and maybe have been kidnaped by the hermit and tied up. Then I would have chewed off my ropes or rubbed them off on a bit of broken glass. The idea really didn't appeal to me.

I helped Aunt Bessie get supper ready, and there was still no sign of Uncle Rufus. We set the table, and I put ice in the glasses. Aunt Bessie told me to go ahead and pour the tea because he would be along any minute.

Well, at last he did come. He gave us each a big hug when he came in.

"Did you talk to him?" Aunt Bessie asked.

"Did you catch him? Was it a pipe?" I asked him.

"Slow down, you two. I'm outnumbered." He smiled when he said it, then looked at me and frowned as though he were perplexed, then seemed to make himself relax again. "Let's set down for victuals," he suggested. "I'll tell you about it."

Over dinner, he said, "Well, we checked out the place, and we couldn't find no sign of a break-in. We went inside and didn't find any footprints—'course, we checked only the first floor, but I guess if we didn't find any there, we wouldn't find any elsewhere, unless that hermit flew through there.

"Well, then we drove into town, and we knocked on that hermit's door, and he was inside, just pretendin' that he wasn't home, until Hugh got mad and told him to let us in or he'd take the whole house apart, and I called and told him to open up or we'd take things to the police. So he opened up the door, snarling and whimpering by turns, and wanting to know what we were talking about. So I told him."

On this, Uncle Rufus suddenly dug really hard into his meat loaf, as though eating it helped him think about something he couldn't understand. He frowned and ate for a minute or two then said, "Well, after I told him, he looked pretty astonished. Then he up and told us he'd been havin' an interview with one of them reporters and another fellow he didn't know. And Hugh, he called the man a liar, and the hermit went to whimperin' again, and I asked him who the reporter was. He told me it was this woman, Sally Carr, and she was stayin' at the boardin' house and is working as a stringer for a whole bunch of papers."

"What's a stringer?" I asked him.

"Best I can figure is that when a newspaper gets a story in some out-of-the-way place, it'll pay somebody just a tiny salary to keep up with the facts and make reports every now and then. This gal's workin' for a bunch of different papers snoopin' out the facts for them. That's what a stringer does."

He wiped his mouth with his napkin. "Anyway, we rung her up and trooped over to the boardin' house, and she backed up his story all right. Then she said that she had interviewed a farmer from over at Pisgah, too, at the same time as the hermit. And while we was there, she rung this other fellow up on the phone, and he talked to us and said yes, he'd been down just this afternoon and had been back home only a few minutes, having just walked in the door. He said if we went to the p'lice, he'd be glad to come and say his piece and write an affidavit that they'd all been together. Well, that old hermit, he just fell apart and started cryin', and thanked the man over the phone, and said folks always did treat him bad, and he was going to go to his grave an old and broken man. He's got a right odd voice—high and trembly, like maybe he's too high strung and nervous. So, we got back in the truck and left. The man's got hisself an alibi, and there ain't nothing we can say to that."

I felt crushed. "Don't you believe me?" I asked.

"I believe somebody at the house rushed at you and scared you, Jean. Maybe it was the hermit and maybe not—it sure might have been somebody tryin' to look like the hermit."

"It was the hermit," I said. "You said it yourself—his voice is so high and trembly. That's why I got so scared when he yelled, because it was almost a shriek, like what you would hear from a ghost story."

"Well, a man's voice can be imitated as well as the rest of him," Uncle Rufus said. "Don't you fret about it, and don't say anything in front of the boys. Hugh doesn't want to worry them."

Chapter Eighteen
The Cave

Robbie and Bruce came sauntering over the hill just after we'd finished up the dishes in the steamy kitchen. Robbie looked pretty happy-go-lucky as usual, and Bruce looked as though he had been made to come. I supposed that he had been.

Bruce came up the steps, and Robbie climbed up over the railings of the porch and swung down with a thump next to me. "You ride Sarge yet?" he asked me. "I bet it was fun. I bet it was almost as fun as my dirt bike. Your uncle won't let me ride him, but maybe he'd let us both ride on him. Why don't you ask him?"

"Answer's already no, Robbie," Uncle Rufus said with a laugh as he came out onto the porch. "You just ain't ready yet. You haven't learned to respect that critter yet."

He thrust out his hand to each boy in turn, then said, "Well, it's turnabout, today. You young'uns set here and I'll fetch out some pie. Jean's our guest of honor tonight, though we been workin' her plenty hard enough by day, I expect."

We all sat down on wooden porch chairs. Robbie's was a rocking chair. He settled back and rocked with a nervous, quick kind of rocking. "I sure want to ride that horse," he said.

"Just leave Mr. Simpson alone about it," Bruce said. "It's not polite to keep yammerin' about it."

"Oh, cool off, Bruce. I ain't yammerin'. I just want to ride him."

Bruce looked away in disgust. Robbie rocked with a pattern of sharp creaking sounds. He just never held still I thought.

"Say, what about the cave?" he asked me. "Have you seen it yet?"

"Uncle Rufus showed it to me."

"We could go in there some day and maybe hunt up that stolen jewel and then get a reward. Maybe those crooks hid it up there. Or maybe we could go in and find a albino crawfish. I ain't ever seen one before, 'cept that one that's pickled in foraldeehyde at school. Doesn't that stuff smell awful? Have you ever seen one?"

"Ain't no jewel up there," Bruce said. "And if you'd keep your mouth shut long enough and set still, you'd get to see an albino crawfish up there. As it is, you never get to see anything because you make too much noise."

"Oh, I don't make so much noise. Say, that pie looks good. Are there seconds? Is that piece for me? Could I have the other one, Mr. Simpson?"

He was saying all this as Uncle Rufus walked out with two pie plates.

Uncle Rufus rapped him on the head with the bottom of one of the pie plates. "Mind yore manners, boy. The big piece is for the guest of honor, my little Jean. You take this piece and be thankful you got any. I'll be out directly, Bruce."

Uncle Rufus and Aunt Bessie came out soon, bringing their pieces and Bruce's piece. We all sat comfortably on the porch, with Aunt Bessie rocking slowly, and Robbie keeping up his rapid-fire rocking. Bruce sat pretty quiet for a while, but Uncle Rufus kept up talking and telling stories, and every now and then he'd say, "Ain't that the way you heard it, Bruce?" and Bruce would answer him, not in his usual curt way either. He'd say, "Why, I guess it is, Mr. Simpson."

By and by Bruce started talking more. He and Uncle Rufus got to talking about old rifles—things called flintlocks and harquebus firers.

"My great-uncle had a pretty good collection," Bruce said. "Some of them guns was over 200 years old and had been on display at museums. Dad's still got a few of them, but the collection was broken up in the dispute over the will."

Then he went to describing them to Uncle Rufus, and Uncle Rufus went inside to get a big full-color book he had of firearms all through history. They sat under the porch light, pointing at the different color plates and talking about the guns. I was over by Aunt Bessie. She dropped her hand onto my head. "You ain't homesick, are you, Jean?" she asked me.

"Oh no," I told her. "Even *I* thought I would be—more than what I am, I mean," I said.

Robbie, full of pie and tired out, was content to keep up his rocking and just listen to us.

I looked up at Aunt Bessie. "I guess this must be my very favorite place to be."

"Ain't quite as scared as you used to be either," she told me. "You've got right comfortable around the dogs, and you can ride Sarge, now."

"It's such a beautiful place," I told her. I looked out over the front lawn. There was a heavy, warm smell of lilacs that hung in the air over the bushes along the front of the house. The big shade tree cast a dimness over the dusky lawn. Out in the distance, the peepers were chirping their soft, rhythmic song: crickets and birds and sleepy sounding insects, all saying good night. Good night, good night. Aunt Bessie's hand touched my neck. "I'm glad you like it here," she said. "A farm just gets into your bones, don't it? That's why we can't give it up. Though sometimes it's a struggle." This last line she said half to herself, and I wondered if everything was okay with the farm.

Robbie piped up. "Hey, were you scared of the dogs and of Sarge? They wouldn't hurt anybody, 'cept jewel thieves."

Aunt Bessie's mind got off the farm, and she said, "Jean's been tryin' to trust the Lord for courage this summer, and she's been comin' right along, I think."

"Say, I bet the best thing for that would be to go into that cave," he said. "If you want to be brave, that's the place. Course, I ain't scared of anything in there, and I know my way all around the place," he boasted. "And I could take you through all by myself. I bet I could."

"You just get a hold of your boasting, young man," Aunt Bessie said. She went on stroking my hair as though her mind had gone back to other things—the farm, probably. But I felt a sudden thrill go over me. I could ride Sarge now and play with the dogs. Maybe the cave really was next. It had scared me a lot the first time I had seen it, but then, so had Babe and Blackie and Sarge. "Maybe Uncle Rufus would take us," I suggested.

"Shoo, who needs a guide. I can get through that cave all right," he said. Just then Uncle Rufus looked up from the book that he and Bruce were poring over, and he said, "Say, Jean, come look at some of these here pictures."

I went over for a look. Bruce was saying, "That there gun's just like the pair of muskets that my dad really prized

the most—the pair he sent to Charleston for their exhibit."
The gun he pointed out looked pretty crude. It had a long,
long barrel, much longer than a rifle barrel. "Course,"
he added, "they been lost some time now. I guess that
my Uncle Angus stole 'em away when he came back from
Scotland." Something clicked in my head. It was starting
to come back to me—the image of what that hermit swung
up to hit or scare Sarge.

"Uncle!" I exclaimed.

He looked up quickly. Bruce, startled by my voice,
looked up too. Even Aunt Bessie glanced over. Then I
remembered I wasn't supposed to worry the two boys;
so I just swallowed and said, "I—I've got to tell you
something—later I mean—but the musket reminded me
of something."

"Sure," he said, a little puzzled. After a moment, Bruce
went on talking, and I went back and sat by Aunt Bessie.
But the cool breeze that had started to blow with the
darkness now made me feel cold. That hermit *had* been
in the house.

Aunt Bessie went inside to get a sweater, and Robbie
leaned closer to me. "We could go up to that cave—
tomorrow if you want."

"No," I told him.

"You 'fraidy cat. Watcha think's gonna happen? You
scared of the dark, little girl?"

"Be quiet!" I said.

"You are scared. Whyn't you just admit it."

"Maybe I am and maybe I'm not. It's none of your
business."

"Why'd you come here if you didn't really want to
do anything? What happened to courage? Ain't that what
you wanted?"

"What happened to brains?" I retorted. "Don't you have any? If you do, how come Uncle Rufus won't let you ride Sarge? He lets everybody else."

"Well, I got brains to go through that cave. My Pa lets me go through there, and I been through there plenty of times. You're just a 'fraidy cat. Any old fool can get through that cave. It's nothing—just one passage is all. You can't even get lost."

I leaned forward. "Uncle," I called.

He looked up.

"Could we go to the cave this week?" I asked him. "Will you take me through?"

"Sure 'nough," he promised. "Saturday, first thing. It'll likely take a few hours. Can't spare the time during the week."

Bruce looked up and shook his head. "Don't forget the buyer's coming into town," he told Uncle Rufus.

"That's right. Have to be Saturday after next, honeybun," he said. "I might sell those calves this week, and we do need the money."

Robbie and I glanced at each other. "You'll chicken out in two weeks," he whispered.

"I will not."

"Then if you ain't scared, I dare you to come with me. I *dare* you, chicken little."

I meant to tell him how silly it was to give and take dares. I think it's one of the silliest things in the world. But I knew that no matter what I said, he was going to call me scared again. And I got the idea that once Robbie had found a good name to call you, he'd never let it go. He was always doing things to annoy Bruce.

"I'll let you know," I said at last.

"You come up to our place tomorrow," he said quietly. "Your uncle wants us to show you 'round on the good trails anyway. He wants you to have a chance to hike a lot."

"I said I'll let you know," I told him.

By then it was pretty dark; so the boys said good night and left us. It was then that I told Uncle about the hermit having what I thought was a musket in his hands.

"That's what he was swinging," I said. "It was a long pipe—only really it was the barrel of the musket he was swinging, like it was a club."

He patted my shoulder. "I thought you hadn't seen it very well."

"I just got one glance at it, Uncle, but that's what it was. The metal was really coarse and rough. That's why I thought it was old pipe."

"Well, maybe it was and maybe it wasn't. We won't worry about it right now," he said.

I think the way he treated my discovery bothered me more than he realized. He thought my imagination was running away with me. If he'd bothered to ask Penny, he would have known I don't have any imagination.

I went up to bed and thought about it some more. I figured that I had gone out on a limb to trust him about Sarge. He owed it to me to trust me about the musket. The whole reason I hadn't been sure of the thing in the hermit's hands was that I'd never seen a musket before. I'd never imagined a gun with a barrel that long. But now that I'd seen one, I knew. But Uncle Rufus, just like everyone else, was so used to quiet, timid, chicken Jean that he wasn't going to listen to me.

Before I went to bed, I sat and looked out the window. I thought about the cave and about how nobody took me seriously and about how I wanted to be brave and heroic and about how much I wanted to prove to Bruce that I wasn't green and prove to Robbie that I wasn't scared. I decided to go over to Robbie's the next day after chores. Just to see the cave.

Chapter Nineteen
Plain Fools

The next morning I didn't say anything about the musket. I helped with chores, did the breakfast dishes, and then asked Uncle Rufus if there would be time for me to go over to Maclarans'.

"Sure!" he said with a smile. "Bruce told me that he'd have this morning off. You might get him and Robbie to take you up to the fire tower. I reckon you could make the climb—with a few rests."

"Maybe," was all I said.

"Have Aunt Bessie put you up a lunch," he suggested. "Then hurry on over. No need to be back until this afternoon, if you go hiking."

I didn't have much to say to him, and he looked a little curious, as though puzzled. Aunt Bessie packed me a lunch, and I went up to the road about ten o'clock to walk up to Maclarans'.

Their house was a long, low building, much less a farmhouse than Uncle Rufus's place. But there was a small, grayed shed that looked like a small barn. Robbie came running out of it as soon as I walked up the drive.

"Yea!" he shouted. "I knew you'd try it!" Then he stopped and put a finger to his lips. "Shhh. Bruce's somewhere around. You go back up the road, and I'll be there in about ten minutes with some stuff we'll need."

Up to that point I still hadn't firmly decided to try the cave, but then the next thing I knew, I was obeying Robbie's directions and was walking silently back up the drive and up the road a little piece to stay out of sight of the house.

It seemed like a long wait for Robbie, but as soon as he came, I saw why he had taken so much time. He was carrying a lunch bag, two yellow hard hats, and an old fashioned lantern that he called a coal miner's lantern.

At least, I told myself, he was pretty well prepared.

"We better hurry up and get off the road," he said.

I glanced at him. "Why? I thought you went up to the cave all the time."

"Sure I do, but I still don't want Bruce going along with us and ruining everything. Come on."

He found a trail that branched off the road, and we followed it uphill.

It was a long walk to the cave. I let Robbie tote most of the stuff. He was just as talkative. He chattered on and on about the cave and caves in general, and what he was going to do when he got older, and how brave he was, and how he wasn't afraid of anything, not even the dark. "And let me tell you," he added, "There ain't nothing darker than the inside of a cave, 'cept maybe the inside of a shark's belly, where I wouldn't want to be." Then he looked at me and grinned. "Still scared?"

"I'm not that scared," I told him.

"Oh, sure you ain't. Well, it don't matter. A cave's a good place to make yourself brave, I reckon."

Then he was off again, talking about dark places and scary places, and other caves that were like mazes. He began to get on my nerves. I guess that when I had first met Robbie Maclaran I had thought him to be friendly and good-natured and lively, but now I realized that he was all talk, and all he would ever do were the things that *he* wanted to do. That was why he talked so much—he didn't want anybody else to be talking.

"Say, I bet you even use a night-light at home," he said. "Come on now, you do, don't you? Ain't that what your aunt was getting at about you tryin' to be braver?"

I finally stopped. "Robbie Maclaran, if you go on one more time about me being afraid of things, I'll go right home!"

"Shoot, you couldn't even find your way," he mocked.

"You just watch me." I turned back around and headed the other way on the trail.

"Oh, come on now, Jean. I'm sorry!" he called. Then he came running after me. "I'm sorry, Jean. I was just teasin'." He got in front of me and stopped me. "I am sorry. Don't go back. We're almost there. I won't call you scared no more."

I was really mad at him and was pretty fed up, too. But he looked like he was sorry and like he felt bad; so I said, "Okay, but I will turn around if you say any more about it."

"I won't. I'm sorry."

We continued on. A long time later, we at last came up the steep part of a hill, and there was the mouth of the cave again. This time my eyes went right to it.

Robbie opened his lunch bag.

"We're going to eat already?" I asked him.

"No, girl! This ain't my lunch. It's stuff for the hats." He pulled a bottle out of the bag and took up one of the hard hats. There was a little cap on the light of the hard hat. He unscrewed it and poured in some liquid.

"These are called carbide lamps on these here helmets. Well, mine's a carbide lamp, anyway, but yours has a 9-volt battery. You got a belt? Good. Hook the battery onto your belt and try the hat on."

I did as he said. It took some adjusting, but when I flicked on the helmet switch, the light was good.

Meanwhile, Robbie had gotten his helmet lit in a way I never would have guessed. After he'd gotten it filled up, he just passed his hand, really roughly, across the front of the light. As his hand cleared it, a flame sprang up. "Now for the lantern," he said as he clamped the hat down on his head and turned to the miner's lantern. I didn't ask him to explain how the friction from his hand had lit the carbide lamp. I didn't want to act like I didn't know anything.

While he worked with the lantern, I looked at the mouth of the cave. It was the darkest thing I had ever seen. I took a few steps into it, then a few more. If I kept my back to Robbie and the sunlight, I faced a wall of darkness with walls of darkness on either side. I flicked on the helmet, but the walls retreated only very little. I could see a few steps in front of me, but that was all. The light breeze that continually played through the cave blew over me, bringing a chill with it. I had been sweating out in the sunlight and now felt cold.

After a moment I couldn't take the closed-in feeling and the blankness of the dark, and I turned around to where I could see the light spilling in from the entrance. It felt good to see that light. How long would it be, I thought, before I would see it again? Uncle Rufus had said something about being a few hours in the cave if I went with him. Hours? It was hard to imagine going down into a rock prison for hours, knowing that there was beautiful sunlight, warm and alive, above the tons and tons of solid rock.

I went back out into the warm afternoon. Robbie lit the lantern. He did it by about the most foolish method I ever saw. After he had gotten the fuel into it and had pumped up a cloth wick with the fumes, he just held the lantern against the light of his own carbide helmet. A tongue of flame shot up from the lantern, and he jerked it away, then turned down the wick. He looked up and laughed at the risk he had taken, but he wouldn't have laughed if that flame had burned his face or hair. I think that it was then that I realized Robbie was a plain fool. He had no sense of risk or of responsibility. He only cared about himself and what he wanted, and even then he wasn't as careful about himself as anybody with sense would be.

I guessed that Robbie was about the most foolish person I'd ever met, but there was a bigger fool there that day. It was me. Knowing what I knew, I still let him lead me into that cave.

Chapter Twenty
The Betrayal

The first several yards of the cave were probably the easiest. The passage was wide enough for a two-lane highway, and—though the roof was low—it wasn't too low for us. We didn't have to stoop. The illusion of being in a closed-in place gradually dwindled for me as we continued to push ahead into the wall of darkness. Obviously, with a breeze on my face and no real barricade before me, I was not being boxed in. It only seemed that way because the darkness was so thick.

Every now and then a bat would zing by, and the first couple times Robbie glanced at me, kind of haughtily, to see if I was cringing. But I felt perfectly sure that the bats would leave us alone. I had already been around them and knew that they were less interested in me than I was in them. I think my first real scare came when Robbie showed me what he called a cave cricket. It looked just like a spider except it had only six legs instead of eight, and it was orange. It was crouched up on the rock roof just above our heads, and I thought it looked like a pretty disgusting creature, but I hid my fear of it.

It was in looking up at the cave cricket that I realized that the roof had come down even lower toward us. Then when I looked back to see the glimmer of light from the entrance, I saw only another wall of darkness. And the funny thing was, this wall of darkness behind me didn't make me feel boxed in. Instead, it made me feel like I was very small and it was very large—like anything at all might come howling up on us through that darkness.

I abruptly turned back around and forced thoughts of the blackness at my back out of my mind. Just the same, it was hard to put my back to such a big unknown. Robbie had been watching me all this time, but he didn't say anything.

We moved ahead, and soon the ground, which was strewn with enormous slabs of rock, became more and more muddy. The slabs of rock beneath our feet became more uneven so that we had to pick our way over and around them. Then, abruptly, we were at the bank of a stream. The bank was all mud or soft earth.

Robbie tried to find a less steep way to get down it, because the bank was about five feet high. But there was no way down it except to slide down, which we did. We got long streaks of mud down our backs from head to heel. We had to wade through the stream because we weren't big enough to get across in one jump. That made me nervous. The stream looked very unstreamlike, probably because there was so much mud flowing through it. There were places that looked very still and very dark, as though they might be pools that were full of pot holes.

Nevertheless, Robbie hopped across through the water, and I followed in his exact steps, guided by the clouds of mud he had stirred up in the water.

"Lookee," he said. He crouched on the bank and stared at the water. I followed his example. There was something greenish-brown in the stream. Robbie splashed at it, and it gave a humping kind of lurch and a throb of its gills as it clumsily wiggled away, right past my feet.

I gave a little scream and jumped back. He laughed.

"What was that?" I asked.

"I don't know. Head was like a big frog, but it looked to me like it had a tail. Some kind of cave critter, I guess."

Orange spiders and huge, misshapen frog-things. I didn't like caves. I had decided that much. I wanted to go back outside. The boxed-in feeling came back and hit me like a wall. My knees felt weak.

Robbie straightened up. "Ready to go on?" he asked.

"Sure." But my voice didn't even convince me.

We took stock of the bank. The roof came down like a dome in front of us. The stream itself petered out into a narrow little brook on the west wall of the cave. It disappeared under a narrow ledge. So we walked upstream, following the bank. Robbie kept inspecting the wall, looking for a passage, but then when we got far enough upstream, he said, "Now I remember better. We follow the stream through a passage that gets real tight. We're gonna have to walk right through the stream part of the way."

I didn't like that. I wondered if there were any more "cave critters" in the stream and what they might do to my feet as I walked through their homes. In fact, I almost told Robbie that I wanted to go back, but then I thought about going home to Uncle Rufus with my clothes all muddy. He'd likely be mad, because he would know that I knew perfectly well that I should have told him we were going to the cave. I really didn't want to have both Uncle Rufus and Robbie mad at me; so I talked myself into going further just a little bit. Likely, Robbie's footsteps ahead of mine would chase any stream dwellers further upstream.

Soon enough the walls came in a lot closer and the roof bowed down. The stream became much narrower, and the banks got too steep to walk on. Finally the banks and the walls just joined, and the roof was down really low. We had to crab-walk, with one foot on one side of the narrow stream, and one foot on the other side, and our bodies crouched way down and bent forward. Thus we waddled forward, one foot taking a step, then every ounce of weight shifting over to it so that the other foot could take a step, all this in a low stoop with our helmets scraping the roof. With the glare of the helmets and the coal miner's lantern on us, we looked like curious, low-slung cave monsters ourselves.

This tortured walk took an incredibly long time, and not just because we were moving slowly, either. The stream passage wound back and forth, back and forth, like a ribbon or a switchback.

At last, when my knees and ankles were bundles of pain, and my back ached from being bent, Robbie gave me a hand up the right side of the bank. I realized that it had begun to slope more gradually, and that the right wall had receded again. We walked at a stoop for several paces, leaving the stream behind, and at last came to a wide place that was clear. After the crowded, closed-in stream passage, this room seemed like a very open place. Robbie called it the lunch room, and we celebrated our arrival by sharing my lunch. I had carried it all that way in my belt, so the sandwiches were a little smashed, but I didn't care. Robbie had a canteen hooked onto his belt, and we drank water out of that.

Afterward, I carefully folded up the wrappers from the lunch and the brown paper bag and tucked the packet into my belt. I would throw it out later.

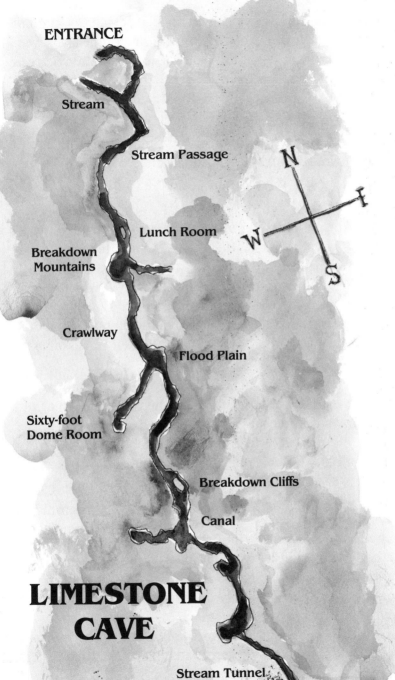

The Betrayal

ENTRANCE

Stream

Stream Passage

N
E
W
S

Lunch Room

Breakdown
Mountains

Crawlway

Flood Plain

Sixty-foot
Dome Room

Breakdown Cliffs

Canal

LIMESTONE
CAVE

Stream Tunnel

We followed the passage until it came to a solid mountain of broken slabs of stone. Some of the slabs were bigger than Uncle Rufus. The jagged mountain looked like it went clear up to the roof, which was considerably higher here. I was actually disappointed.

"Is that all?" I asked.

He gave me a look of disgust. "Course not. This here's breakdown, that's all. We got to climb along it."

"Climb? But it goes right up to the roof!"

"Come on, I'll show you!"

He started climbing up it. I felt afraid, but I followed him. As we climbed up, he began inching his way to the left. I couldn't tell how he could find the passage, because the enormous cave-in of rock went right up to the roof and was spread to the walls on either side. Certainly, there were many dark fissures here and there, but I couldn't tell one from another, and they all looked impassable to me.

Nevertheless, we inched our way forward and to the left, toward the western wall, and then I realized that the breakdown did not meet the roof all the way around. The enormous pile of broken rock looked like a wall from the front, but as you came around a spur of it, you realized that it was more like a mountain. We went right to the top (I didn't look down) and, really, the footing was not hard to find. Then we came around, dropping lower to get good footing, then climbed up to roof level again, then came lower again as we continued along the side of the mountain. It was exhausting work, and pretty soon I realized that there was only one way over this breakdown, and that Robbie had it memorized. A newcomer to the cave might get all the way to the bottom of the pile and seek a passage along the opposite cave wall, where there was none. Or he might go all the way to the top of the

114

pile and conclude that it had blocked up the whole cave. Or he might spend hour upon hour poking his nose into some of the fissures between rock and ceiling, and still not find a way to get through.

At last we started our descent, and I realized that we were coming into another large room.

"This here place is the confusing one," Robbie said. I was already confused. I felt that—left to myself—I never would even be able to find my way back over the breakdown mountain. From here on in, I was stuck with Robbie, because I could never get back by myself. "Let me see if I c'n recall where that next passage is," he told me. "We got to hunt for it."

He poked around the smooth wall on the far side of the room, but I inspected down the length of the huge breakdown pile. In this room, the western wall was solid, and the eastern wall was all breakdown. I searched along the eastern wall, trying to help him find the way. You see, in a cave, the passages aren't perfectly hollowed out like tunnels. A wall might have all kinds of crawlways or nooks in it that look like they lead somewhere but don't. And then it might have just a tiny crack in it that looks like nothing, but if you poke your head in it and keep going, you'll find it's the passage you've been looking for.

That's kind of what happened to me. I found a crack and looked at it, then realized when I got my face down to it that it wasn't a crack between two slabs in the breakdown at all but a real opening. I shone my light into it, letting darkness spring up all around me for a minute, and saw that after a narrow squeeze, it opened up into a tunnel among the broken and tilted slabs of rock. I pushed my shoulders forward for a better look, curious in spite of my fear. I saw that after a few yards the breakdown gave way to smooth rock tunnel. The walls seeped with moisture. I wondered if some part of the stream had once wended through there.

I pulled my head out and glanced back at Robbie, who was against the far wall with the lantern.

"I think I found it," I called to him.

"No, you haven't," he said back. "It's over here. Come on."

So I joined him, and he was right. There was a narrow, low gap under a ledge in the western wall. Robbie squeezed through. I stuck my head in and realized that the roof did not rise at all in here. Robbie was snaking his way through on his belly.

"Doesn't the roof get any higher?" I asked him.

"Further on," he grunted. "Come on!"

I played with the idea of staying right there and waiting for him, but even then, when I glanced at the room I was in, I realized that it was swamped in darkness again. Without Robbie's coal miner's lantern and additional helmet light, I would be in a dark prison. And if my light should go out, I would be lost in complete darkness, unable to even see my hand in front of my eyes. I shuddered and squeezed through.

This belly crawling also lasted a long time. I soon caught up with him, but it wasn't much comfort, because his feet were in front of my face. We continued inching our way along, and it seemed to me that he was going incredibly slow, as though he enjoyed keeping me back in this narrow, tight prison, or as though it hadn't entered his head that I wasn't enjoying myself.

"Would you hurry up?" I demanded.

"Okay, okay, simmer down," he said.

I couldn't even lift my head without the roof stopping me. It was like being crushed by an enormous hand. The sensation got worse and worse, and just as it seemed that I would shout out again for Robbie to get me out of here, I heard him say, "There it is." I realized that my eyes were closed and opened them. He was on his knees ahead of me. After a moment more of crawling I found that I could get on my knees, too, and lift my head.

We crawled forward and then stood up. I lifted my helmet and wiped sweat off my face.

Ahead of us, the stream had returned. It had turned into a kind of flood plain. As we looked ahead and my eyes adjusted to the cave's dimensions, I realized that one passage was going off to the right (or southeast) and another was going off to the left (due west). Robbie took the one going toward the right.

We soon came to another mountain of breakdown, but this one was lower than the first. It didn't come anywhere near the roof. At first that made me feel better, but pretty soon I realized that this mountain of breakdown was even worse than the other. For one thing, the broken slabs of rock that made it up were much bigger, and there were larger gaps between them. Also, they were not all anchored down. I stepped on the edge of one flat piece of rock and felt it sink under me as the other end came up. I leaped ahead in time to avoid capsizing it.

I had no idea how Robbie was finding his way. In half a dozen places the breakdown mountain edged down toward the wall of the cave, as though there might be a passage down there. It did not have a front end and a back end; rather, it was a many-armed octopus of a mountain, and somehow, we were finding our way along the correct arms of it.

"The canal is ahead," Robbie said. "Feel any braver yet?"

"I just feel tired. We've got to rest at the canal, Robbie. I don't think I can go on."

"You can rest all you want up ahead," he told me.

At last he led me down one side of the boulders and jagged rocks, and there, sure enough, was a wide canal. I stepped up to the edge and looked at it. It was shallow and very wide. But somebody, sometime, had obviously moored a boat there. A rope, staked into the dirt on the bank, floated idly in the slow current.

"Boat ain't much good in here," Robbie said. "Unless some naturalist was trying to catch something out of one. I'll see if I can find some stepping stones. There might be deep places in the canal in spots."

He walked away and I looked out across the canal again. There was a steep bank on the other side, not made up of dirt but rather of more cliff-like rocks. I scanned the opposite bank as well as I could in the cone-shaped beam of my helmet light. It looked to me like a pretty sheer bank that would be climbed only with difficulty. "Robbie," I said. "Do you mean you want to go over there and try to climb along that cliff?"

He didn't answer me. I looked back at him, but there was only darkness there, darkness and the pale beam of my light. I turned around and looked the other way. Again, nothing. Only darkness. And the darkness away from the water was much more solid, much less reflective than the canal.

A terrible pang of fear went through me, and even then, my very first fear was touched with the aloneness of the place. I was alone.

"Robbie!" I screamed.

There was no answer.

Chapter Twenty-one
Lost

At first I thought that maybe he was just playing a joke on me and had hidden, but as the seconds and then minutes ticked by, I realized that he was gone.

How he had slipped away so quickly, I did not know. The idea that there might be an exit nearby suggested itself. But there was no way to know. I tried walking down the canal, but soon the bank became much more cliff-like, and I realized that it would take a lot of time to continue any new exploration either up or down the canal.

And I knew that time was one thing I didn't have. My battery wouldn't last forever. And if it went out before I got out, the darkness would roll over me like water. I would never find my way out in darkness. To try to define passage entrances with only my hands would take the rest of my life, and probably I would fall off the pile of breakdown if I ever even got to it.

No, I couldn't risk the unknown. I had to go back the way I had come. But even that sent a chill through me. How many times had I felt confused on the way in here? Getting back might take hours, and—as far as my light was concerned—those would be numbered.

Even with the light of my helmet on, the darkness felt twice as huge and oppressive as it had felt with another person nearby. I had read accounts of people lost in caves who had felt themselves ready to die of despair, and suddenly I knew what they had meant. The loneliness, the huge silence, the awful darkness, it was all full of despair.

With blackness crowding me at my back, I went back up to where the bank was muddy. It didn't take me long to find the place where we had climbed down the cliff-like rocks to the beach of the canal. Here was where I felt my first sense of relief. There were traces of mud on the rocks here and there—traces from our own ripple-soled tennis shoes. I began the laborious climb upward, and I wondered if God was helping me get out.

Of course, then I felt awful, because I knew I had gone into this cave without telling anybody just because I was mad at Uncle Rufus and Bruce Maclaran. Then as I climbed a little more, I realized that I had been mad at the world. I'd been out to prove something to everybody. It seemed in my big search for courage, that I'd managed to leave praying for it and watching God work things out for me pretty far behind. Here I was, mad at everybody, and cut off from help, and stranded by a boy who I'd realized I shouldn't have trusted.

I pulled myself up and began going over the top of the hill of breakdown on my feet, with a lot of help from my hands. Now it was up to my mind to try to play everything back in reverse—every landmark, every passage entrance, everything. It sent a thrill of fear through me, because I didn't think I could.

I stayed absolutely still for a minute and tried to think. The best thing to do was to try to rethink things one step at a time. We had walked through the flood plain to get to this hill of breakdown. So I had to look for the rock flood plain with the low, standing water on it. I couldn't shin down the breakdown to the stream or to the wall, just to the wide, wet rock floor.

Of course, all this time I was sweating hard because I was so scared, and I felt the darkness over me like a menace. But I did keep my head, and if I followed an arm of the big slabs of breakdown that deadended into the cave wall, I would just find my way back and start over again. It was tedious, slow work, and I got the idea that my light wasn't as strong as it had been, but I kept going.

Suddenly, abruptly, the breakdown mountain ended in a sheer drop. Down below, water glistened off plains of wide, flat rock. Somehow I had found it.

I didn't even think of everything I had done wrong, I just put my head down on my arms and thanked God that He had gotten me to it. And I asked Him to get me out of that cave.

Carefully, I climbed down the face of the cliff. I followed the flood plain for a good long while. I think I had gone into some kind of daze from relief, because after several minutes I pulled up short and gave myself a little shake. I had not been concentrating on retracing my steps—I had simply been walking.

I went further ahead, and it seemed to me that the walk over the flood plain had not been this long. Up ahead I heard a muffled sound, and I didn't know what it was.

Cautiously, I picked my way over the broken floor of the flood plain. It was slippery in places. I didn't remember having such a difficult time before, either.

I picked my way around a bend, and the noise was getting louder. As I came around the wall, I saw before me a room like a cathedral, with a cataract of water pouring down right in the center.

I looked up, but my light couldn't pierce to the roof here.

The sight frightened me. I had never seen this before. How had I come here? And worse, after a walk around the cataract, I realized that this room was a perfect dead end. The only way out of it was the way I had come into it.

Had I taken a dead-end passage? But where had I taken the wrong turn? My mind went back to the mountain and cliffs of breakdown. Perhaps there were several rock flood plains surrounding it, and I had missed the right one.

I started back, but then my mind suddenly found a possible reason.

When Robbie and I had come to the flood plain, I had noticed that the plain stretched out in two directions. We had gone to the right. Perhaps, in coming back, I had missed the turnoff and had simply continued into the left-hand passage.

I walked along the flood plain. If that were the case, then the turnoff that had brought us into the flood plain region would be on my right as I returned towards it.

I had to stop and inspect the wall several times when crags and ledges appeared in it. A long time ago in school I had read about caves being formed by water. The water had made formations in the harder rock, called flowstone. Many of the deceptive patterns on the walls of the cave were flowstone formations.

I saw a low ledge in the wall up ahead and told myself that probably at one time there had been a perfect little waterfall there; the edge of it was so rounded and polished. Then I realized that this ledge went back quite a way into the wall, which was recessed here. I got down on my hands and knees and looked. First I saw just blank wall, but as my eye followed it along, I realized that it was receding farther and farther. I crawled on hands and knees, each moment expecting the wall to come to a dead end.

It got a lot lower, and soon I was on my stomach, with my head down, inching forward. I wanted to cry again, because I realized that I had found the passage.

Part of the way through, I had to stop to pray. For one thing, I was exhausted, and for another, the darkness was pushing in on me again. I knew I was alone and that there was a long way to go.

During this long crawl, my strength felt like it was slowly oozing out of me. I forced my way on in that narrow, crushed place, but I promised that whenever this thing emptied out into another passage, I was going to rest.

At last I dragged myself into a place where my light beam vanished way ahead in darkness, with no glare to tell me that the roof was right on my head. I groped my way out of the crawlway and cautiously stood up. I played the light beam around to see where I was.

It was a vast room, full of smooth indented rocks and breakdown here and there. But the wall opposite me was unmistakable. It was the first breakdown mountain, and it looked even higher and more impenetrable than before.

Chapter Twenty-two
More Danger

I had meant to rest, but in that vast room, my weak light was haunting, and I was afraid that it would go out soon. I set my hands against some of the jagged edges of the toppled slabs of rock, and was just about to begin what seemed like the hopeless job of finding my way to the next passage, when I heard voices coming.

A search party? I wondered. How long had I been gone? Time was hard to reckon in a cave, but if we had spent an hour coming in, I had spent at least twice that trying to find my way out. Still, that only made three hours all together.

But, there was Bruce. If he had thought of Robbie taking me to the cave, or if he had caught Robbie and somehow popped the truth out of him, he might come to find me. I suddenly realized that Bruce, for all his frowning and abrupt way with words, had never meant me any harm and had been trying to steer me clear of Robbie.

Then it struck me again that Bruce was the only one in his family who had ever professed faith in Christ openly, and that he was the only one interested in spiritual things, as Uncle Rufus said. Perhaps Bruce had looked to me as somebody he had something in common with, somebody whom he had accidentally offended. The memory of his honest apology came back to me. He had wanted to be friends. I knew that I should have overlooked his blunt way of putting things. After all, I really was green.

While I was thinking all this, the voices were getting louder, but I heard a woman's voice, too. Surely not Aunt Bessie. And then there floated down to me a voice that I had heard only once before, and then it had been in a scream. But Uncle Rufus had described it as a high, tremulous voice—the hermit.

I switched off my light and was enveloped in total blackness. But in another second, a dim glow appeared above me. The hermit and some other people were coming.

Groping with both hands, I felt my way back along the floor and almost into the low passage where I had come from. But that was no good. What if they meant to go that way themselves? Once they got into there, they would be sure to see my feet ahead of them, or at least to hear me.

As I said, there were hollowed-out places along the wall, even along the bottom of the wall, where water once had flowed and smoothed out indentations. My hands felt along the smooth wall until I came to one of these indentations. It was long enough for me to squeeze into, and it was in a back corner of this room. If they didn't come poking around, I would be safe.

I had to take off my helmet to do it, but the floor was broken up too, so I let the helmet lie in a low place on the room floor, and I squeezed myself into the long, low indentation. Of course, once I got into it, I couldn't see anything, and I didn't dare poke my head out to look at anything, because they might see me. I just stayed where I was, sheltered in the wall of rock, with the room still pitch dark because they hadn't come down yet. Finally, their voices were suddenly clearer, and I knew they were coming down the side of the mountain of breakdown. I prayed for them just to find the low passage right away without having to search the room for it.

To my dread, a headlamp beam flashed on the wall of breakdown across from me, as though they were coming this way. But it didn't come sweeping toward me or toward my helmet. Their voices went on talking, and I guessed that there were three of them in the big room. I was really scared of that hermit. Whatever he was up to, it was certainly no good.

Suddenly, their voices were muffled again, and the beam from the headlamp went dark as though it had been switched off. That didn't make sense, because if he'd turned back around the way he should have, the beam would have swept around somehow, too.

After a moment in the blackness there was only silence; so I crept out, put on my helmet, and switched it on. I walked back up the room, inspecting the mountain of breakdown. I had to get out, now, because they were in here, too, somewhere. Somehow, my sense of utter solitude slacked off, even though I knew they were enemies. At least they were *people;* and if I had to avoid them, at least I knew I wouldn't fall apart from being completely alone.

Resolutely, I started climbing up the breakdown. The best plan just seemed to be to try to stay at the top of the mountain as best as I could, and only come down where the top of the mountain was impassable for some other reason. Coming into the cave, I had been confused because everything had looked like the opening of a passage, but now as I worked my way over and around the mountain, I realized that at no time had Robbie led me through any of the gaping holes in the pile of broken rocks. We had always stayed with the breakdown under our stomachs or under our feet, and the smooth rock wall had always been across from our backs.

My only fear was that if I climbed around the breakdown mountain too far, I would either make a complete circle and end up where I had started, or at the least, I would end up far from the passage that would guide me out. You see, breakdown is merely rubble all piled up, and a pile of rubble doesn't start or end anyplace. You merely come down it at this place or that place. I could only hope that if I inched around the breakdown mountain too far, that it would be stopped by a solid wall of the cave, and that I could climb down and find myself in the same big room as the passage that had led us to the breakdown.

The climb did seem to be taking me a lot longer than it had coming in. But I couldn't be sure if my memory were playing tricks on me. And even if my memory was correct, it was possible that I was taking longer because I was so tired and so unfamiliar with the climb.

Just as I was pondering on whether or not I should retrace my steps and explore more, I heard a tremendous halloo that sent my heart into my socks. Then suddenly: "Jean! Jean!"

"Uncle Rufus! Uncle Rufus!" I screamed back. "Help me!"

There was an awful moment of silence, and all I could feel was my heart pounding. Then I heard it again: "Jean!"

"I'm here!" I called out. "Uncle!"

I heard rocks rattling and then silence. Suddenly a light popped out, almost directly above me, and in a moment it was followed by Uncle Rufus's face.

Chapter Twenty-three
New Courage

"I'm sorry," was the first thing I said to him.

"You just let me help you outta' here, and then we'll talk about this," he said, kind of sternly, but in the next second he was reaching down. "This is the best way out. Come on."

He helped me over the breakdown, and I followed him down the other side. He led me right to the passage where Robbie and I had eaten lunch earlier.

"Can you go any further?" he asked, squinting at me.

"We have to," I said. "Those people are here."

He looked at me, and for some reason he seemed a little alarmed. "What people, Jean?"

I was too tired to explain. "A group of them," I said wearily. "They just disappeared, but they'll come back, I think. We've got to get out."

"Sure, now," he said, kind of soothing. "We'll do that." He put his arm around my shoulders. "Don't you be afraid while yore old Uncle Rufus is here, honey-bun. Let's go."

We came to the stream passage, and I tried to crab walk out after him, but it was an awfully long way to go, and my legs were sore down to the bones and joints. I'd never been so tired in my life. A couple times I had to stop and rest my hands down on either of the steep banks, just to take the weight off my legs for a second or two.

"Not far, now," he told me. "You're all tuckered out. Sure, that's all. Been scared, too. Right bad scare, I guess. You'll be all right."

At long, long last we came out of the stream passage and walked along the stream itself to the place where Robbie and I had crossed earlier. I saw my own shoe print in the mud.

Uncle Rufus helped me up the opposite bank. Holding on to him for support, I walked up the wide, low passageway, over the crazily tilted slabs of rock on the floor of the cave. Far ahead, I saw pale light thrown against one wall of the cave, and across from that, the even brighter light of the entrance. I started to cry.

I thought it was probably time for Uncle Rufus to start telling me how wrong it was to run off like I had done and go to the cave, and how I had disobeyed and that he was shocked. But instead he just let me cry, and he kept his arms around me, and it felt so good to know he was there, because I had been so scared in that cave.

We stood right in front of the cave entrance, out in the good clean air, and when I looked up again, I realized that it was much later than I had thought. The sun was on the decline. It was at least five in the evening, maybe six.

"Are you all right now?" he asked me.

I nodded.

"You've had a bad scare," he said. I nodded.

"And I'm sorry," I told him. "I'm sorry, Uncle Rufus. I won't ever do it again. I won't ever do anything like this again. I won't. I promise."

"Tell me what you did when you realized you'd been left alone in there," he said gently.

"I got scared. And I called for Robbie. And then I started back the way I had come, only I came to another room instead, a room with a waterfall in the middle of it. The water just came pouring down the middle of it."

He nodded. "That's right. That's the sixty-foot dome room."

He seemed relieved. I continued. "So I went back and kept a better watch, and I think the Lord just guided me to the passage. I went through that, and then I came into the next room. That was when I heard the people."

"Did you *see* the people?" he asked.

"No, just their lights." Suddenly, I realized what he was getting at. He was thinking I'd been seeing things in the cave. "Uncle!" I exclaimed.

"What?" he asked.

"I did not imagine them! Three people came into the room, but I hid from them, and then they left."

"Why did you hide?" he asked.

"One was the hermit. I could tell from his voice. Another was a woman's voice. The other was a man's voice, but I didn't recognize it."

He still looked a little doubtful, and I got indignant. "A person would have to be *hysterical* to imagine that!" I exclaimed. "I was not hysterical! I was finding my way back and was thinking perfectly straight!"

He nodded and then shot a look at me. "Bruce caught hold of Robbie, all soaking wet, and wanted to know what he'd been up to. Robbie teased him with it for a good while, and then finally told him just before supper. Bruce called me right away, and I set out for you. Your aunt's a good deal upset."

I looked down. "I was wrong. I was mad. I just wanted to prove something. I'm sorry."

"I ought to spank you, I reckon, except what you been through was far worse than anything I would do. I guess you been punished, and I guess maybe you see where you been wrong. Sounds like it, anyway. But I trusted you, honey-bun. You let me down, and you broke faith with me."

I looked down on this. "I know," I said. "I know. I wanted to prove to Robbie that I wasn't scared, and I wanted to prove to Bruce that I wasn't green."

"Jean, courage ain't godliness!" he exclaimed. "Courage ain't obedience. There's three great things—faith, hope, and love. Courage ain't even one of them. There's been plenty of brave men who were bad men, but there ain't ever been a man that had those three things that was anything else but a God-fearing Christian. Your aunt and I love you, and it isn't because you're brave or not brave. It's just because we love you. And we knew you wanted to stay here, and we wanted you to. Look at me."

I looked up at him and started to cry again, but he put his arms around me, and said, "You're gonna have to earn back my trust, Jean, but I love you right now."

I nodded and buried my face in the crook of his arm and cried. After a while he said, "Let's go home, honey-bun."

Chapter Twenty-four
I Surprise Uncle Rufus Again

Aunt Bessie didn't fuss when I came in with Uncle Rufus. She just looked at him, and he gave a little nod and said, "She's all right and we've had a little talk."

I told Aunt Bessie I was sorry. She hugged me and kissed me and said there wouldn't be any more fuss that night. I had a cold supper and a hot bath and then went to bed. I was so tired I didn't wake up till almost noon the next morning.

When I realized that I'd missed chores, tears started trickling down my face as I hurried to get dressed. It was the first time I hadn't met Uncle Rufus first thing in the morning. Just as I ran out into the hall, he came up the steps.

"There you are," he said kindly. "Come downstairs and let's chat. I hope you're feelin' better."

"Yes," I said, wiping the tears away and following him downstairs.

"Well," he told me when we got down to the living room. "I been thinkin' some more of this courage business, Jean."

"Yes sir?" I asked.

"You know," he said, "you told me about praying for an adventure. I think the Lord did answer that for you, and I think that one reason that you were able to face things like the dogs and the horses and the time away from home was because—instead of seeing the courage you wanted—you were seeing the Lord at work, answering your prayers."

I nodded. He was right.

"See, I told you that courage came with trust. And as long as you had your trust, or hope, in the Lord, you got the courage as you needed it. But I think when you got fixed on the courage itself and disobeyed the Lord, you lost the ability to be brave. You see, Jean, obedience is all a part of love. Trust is a part of love. You have to love the Lord most of all and be willing to obey and trust Him, and when you do, anything that the Lord has called you to do—like maybe be brave—He can enable you to do."

"Yes sir," I said.

"Now you don't need to fuss about yesterday anymore. You been chastised and you learned a lot. Your aunt and I both love you. Like I said, I'll need to change a few things until I feel sure you won't go off half-cocked any more, but you're a good girl, Jean, just kind of foolish for having let Robbie talk you into anything."

"You won't send me home?" I asked him.

"No. I'll be frank. I had thought about it. I'd worried that you might be too flighty, and we'd always be out heartsick lookin' for you. But I think I know you better than that. I guess I'd call yesterday's episode an exception and not the rule."

I nodded, hopeful.

"However," he said, letting the word roll out. "If you ride Sarge, you got to ride him in the fenced pasture, in sight of the house. And if you go hikin', it's got to be with me or with a person I know and give permission for. You can't just stroll around anymore. I want to know exactly where you are, all the time, until I see that you do have the sense I hope you have."

"Yes sir," I said. I was starting to get the idea that being responsible and dull like I had been was a lot better than being brave.

"We got to give back that hard hat to the Maclarans," Uncle Rufus said. "You want me to take it over?"

"I'd like to go," I said. "I want to talk to Bruce—thank him for finding out about me."

He looked at me a moment, and I think he realized that I felt pretty bad for the way I had thought about Bruce.

"Sure," he said. "Let's go."

We went out to the pickup. I was so humbled and so regretful of everything I had done that I never even thought about how mad I was at Robbie. I had been so upset about the way I'd treated Uncle Rufus and Aunt Bessie that I had almost forgotten about Robbie's role in all this.

You would think that a person who'd been so sincerely sorry for disobeying would stay out of trouble. But as we pulled into the Maclarans' driveway and I got out of the truck, the front door burst open and Robbie came tearing down the steps.

"Hey look; it's the chicken! I see you got out of the cave. Well, don't you feel a lot braver now? Did it take you a long time? I figured it would be pretty easy—"

I'd never punched a person in my life, and so I guess you might have called it beginner's luck when I let loose with a straight punch that knocked Robbie Maclaran off

his feet. He opened his mouth and let out a long cry, and I hit him again.

That was when Uncle Rufus grabbed me and pulled me back and yelled, "Jean! Jean Derwood!"

"I'll show you who's a chicken, you crybaby sneak!" I heard myself yelling. "You let me go, Uncle Rufus, and I'll hit him again! He deserves it!"

Bruce came dashing out the front door, mouth open in astonishment. At sight of him, the one and only flash of martial spirit I've ever felt died in me. Here I was sorry for how I'd treated Bruce, and I started things off by knocking down his little brother.

I just stood there, blankly, and Robbie went running into the house, yelling something and choking back a cry.

"Ain't you ashamed of yourself, young lady?" Uncle Rufus exclaimed.

"Well," Bruce drawled, "Since she did it, I'm glad that at least I saw it. Dad licked him last night, but I don't think Dad quite got the point across about leavin' people in caves like she just did."

"I'm sorry," I stammered to Uncle Rufus. "Suddenly when I saw that he was still treating it like a joke, I just got really mad. I lost control of myself. I'm sorry. I didn't even know I could punch like that!"

He sounded resigned. "Get in the truck, young lady. Here's the hard hat, Bruce. We'll see you later."

"Thanks," Bruce said. He glanced at me, and there was the trace of a smile on his face before he walked away.

Uncle Rufus climbed into the truck and slammed the door and didn't say anything. We pulled out in silence and drove most of the way in silence. I felt wretched.

"Are you going to punish me?" I asked him.

"Mmf," he said. "Your nerves must be shot. I'm going to make you rest, I think. I just ain't never heard of a little bitty thing like you, gentle as you are, hauling off and slugging a boy a head taller than you."

Then he didn't say anything else. We pulled into the farm. Aunt Bessie came out on the porch to meet us, and at the sight of Uncle Rufus's face and then mine, she said, "Lands, what's wrong with you two?"

Uncle Rufus looked at me and said, "She—" And then he looked at Aunt Bessie and then back at me. "Jean here," he began, then looked back at me like he was sizing me up, still trying to figure out how I'd done it.

"What?" Aunt Bessie asked.

Suddenly he slapped his thigh. "She knocked down Robbie Maclaran," he exclaimed, "And gave him a black eye!" Then he bent forward and laughed and laughed and laughed.

Aunt Bessie was horrified. "Jean Derwood!" she exclaimed. "And here you are, laughing!" she said to him.

"It weren't right, Bessie, but it was the funniest thing you ever saw!"

Without a word, I marched into the house to help with supper. The whole time I worked, I could hear Uncle Rufus laughing in the next room.

Chapter Twenty-five
True Courage

Uncle Rufus explained to me that the reason Robbie had disappeared so quickly from the cave was that the canal did lead out. A person had to wade through it upstream and then swim underwater and under a rock ledge, but it wasn't too hard if the time was high summer and water was low. In the spring the current was a lot stronger.

For a few days the subject of the cave was still a little tender to talk about, and we mostly didn't.

Then on Saturday Uncle Rufus walked into the house and found me in the kitchen.

"I was down to the old hunting lodge," he greeted me with. One of the calves got loose, and I chased it down there. While I was pushing through the scrub lookin' for it, I found something."

He went into the living room and came back with a long pipe in his hands, then held it up. It was a musket. You could see it had lain outside for several days, but the condition of it wasn't too bad. The wooden parts of it were still there, partly rotted from the century or so of wear.

"Reckon I'll call up Hugh Maclaran," he said. "You was right, Jean. I should have listened to you."

I just nodded, and he called up Mr. Maclaran.

"So that hermit was in the house somehow," Uncle Rufus said after he had spoken on the phone. "Hugh's coming over."

"Should we tell him about the hermit being in the cave?" I asked.

He shrugged. "It just doesn't mean anything, Jean. Why would he bust into the house, and how did he do it? The bolts and fastenings was secure on everything. And why did that reporter lie to help him?"

"Maybe that was her in the cave," I suggested. "Maybe they know each other somehow."

He shrugged. "Ain't a crime to go into a cave," he said. Just then Aunt Bessie came bustling in from the garden, where she'd been picking tomatoes for lunch.

"You two have long faces," she observed.

Uncle Rufus told her what had happened. Just then Mr. Maclaran came by with Bruce. Mr. Maclaran was a broad, big man, with dark hair and dark eyes. He just squinted at me a little bit when Uncle Rufus introduced us, but he didn't say anything about Robbie or caves or black eyes.

Uncle Rufus filled him in on everything. The powerful, dark-haired man was silent throughout the story; then at last he said, "Doesn't make a lick of sense." Bruce had been fingering the old musket with the attention of a man who loves old guns and their history.

"At least we got it back, Dad," he said.

"It's mate is missing," his father said. "You're right, though, it's better than nothing, but I did love to see them up on the wall together when I was a boy. My favorite pieces."

He frowned and added, "All we can do is keep better watch on the house and make sure that coot stays away from it."

"Be glad to give you a hand," Uncle Rufus said.

"Much obliged."

"What about that cave?" Uncle Rufus asked. "I wonder why the hermit was poking around in there."

Hugh Maclaran glanced at me, a little sourly, and shrugged. "You know—I mean, kids are kids. How do we know it was really the hermit?"

"By his voice," I told him.

"Well, you never did see him. Might have been another woman, or another man with a high voice, for that matter."

He gestured to Bruce, and they stood up with the musket. Uncle Rufus remained thoughtful. "All the same, I think we might go up there ourselves if Jean is willing. That buyer's come and gone. I got some time to spare."

"Suit yourself," the other man said. "Come on, Son."

Bruce glanced at us and left.

Uncle Rufus stayed where he was. "Maclaran can be pretty bullheaded," he observed. "What would you say to another trip to the cave?"

I looked down. I didn't feel ready to go back there. I really didn't want to. But I knew he wanted me to go with him. Then I remembered something.

"Uncle," I said, "I think I did find another passage in that cave."

"Some are dead ends," he told me.

"I know, but it would fit—about the light suddenly disappearing like I told you—if they had ducked into that passage I had found earlier. I'd just thought it was a dead end, too, because Robbie took me down that really low passage, and he thought it was the only one that led out of that room."

"I thought it was, too," Uncle Rufus said. "Course, even a dead-end passage has got its uses, like if folks are hiding something in it or having secret meetings there."

We looked at each other.

"Could I show it to you?" I asked.

"Sure," he said.

Chapter Twenty-six
Trapped

We told Aunt Bessie about going up to the cave, and it wasn't long before we were jouncing over the trail up the mountain.

I wasn't sure what would go through my mind at sight of the cave again, after all that I had gone through the last time I had been there. But, it was like Uncle Rufus said. Courage comes from trust, and trust comes from love. We put on our hard hats, each equipped with a 9-volt battery, and Uncle Rufus hooked a flashlight onto his belt.

Then he took my hand and asked, "Okay so far?"

I looked up at him and nodded. I wasn't very scared at all with him there. We went inside, and the darkness gave me some bad moments, but I was more used to it. By the time we crossed the stream I was pretty well adjusted to the cave-dark and didn't feel so boxed in.

Once again we walked upstream and crab-walked up the narrow, low stream-passage. Then we came to the breakdown mountain. Uncle Rufus was a much different guide from Robbie. He would turn back and shine his head lamp down at my feet to help me find my way, and over the rough spots he would give me his hand.

At last we were climbing down the other side of the breakdown in the next big room. I tried to show him about where I had found the other passage, but we had to search for quite a while. It had been so easy last time—but that was because I'd had no idea what I was looking for. Already my mind had some expectations about what would and would not be the opening of a passage.

Uncle Rufus tugged my elbow and showed me what looked like wet spots on the rocks.

"Wax," he said. "From candles. Must've had a hard time carrying candles in a blowing cave."

"Maybe they used candles the first time they came here," I suggested. "Before they got hard hats."

We followed the wax droppings, and this time I found the narrow hole. I thrust my head inside and looked. I came back out and nodded. He whistled between his teeth. "It sure looks tight."

"I think it gets wider once you get into it—not wide enough to stand, and maybe not even wide enough to go on hands and knees, but it is a passage of some kind. I think it was there before all this breakdown was here, and then the breakdown hid it. The tight spot is trying to squeeze around the breakdown rocks."

"Well, let's try it," he said.

"I'm littler. Maybe I should go first. That way you can pull me out if I get stuck."

He forced a smile. "If it gets anywhere near that tight, then there ain't nobody who could get through. Okay, try it."

I squeezed all the way into it. For a moment it was so tight that I thought I was already stuck, but then I managed to inch ahead around the jagged edges of the rock slabs and just keep squeezing through. I don't know how Uncle Rufus ever made it, but he did. Then suddenly the passage was higher, though narrow. Then it got wider, and I was able to get on hands and knees. I heard Uncle Rufus scrambling after me. Though it was hard to be sure, I guessed that the walls of the crawlspace weren't flowstone. They somehow looked manmade, and I wondered if somebody had hollowed this place out with a pick. It would have been a huge job to do. We crawled on hands and knees for a long time.

I gradually became aware that the crawlspace was gently sloping downward. I looked back up the tunnel, past Uncle Rufus, and saw that we had been going downward for some time.

My knees got sore from all the crawling. Still, it went on, then suddenly I stopped, and Uncle Rufus almost fell into me. "Look!" I exclaimed. He looked up at the ceiling of the tunnel. A crossbeam of wood had been placed there. We crawled on.

The tunnel became higher and the descent got a lot steeper. We stood up and continued the walk downhill. Now we passed wooden support beams every few yards. This was plainly some manmade shaft, but it was a very old one. Uncle Rufus scratched his head. "Well, I'd heard about a secret hideout for Unionist sympathizers!" he exclaimed. "But I sure didn't know their escape tunnel was digged up into the blowing cave!"

I glanced at him. He smiled. "During the Civil War there was plenty of high feeling for the Union, even in the heart of the South. But Unionists wasn't treated too kindly, especially since most of them was spies. I'd heard that they would hide out in these hills from time to time. This must have been how they got by. Wonder where this thing leads."

We went on walking and soon came to old wooden steps that creaked and groaned as we went down. Some of them were even broken, and we had to step over them.

At last we came to a level earth floor. The wall across from us was perfectly smooth. We shone our lights on it and saw that it was painted brick.

I pushed against it. Uncle Rufus inspected the room where we had come out. It was small and had packed earth walls and support beams, except for the wall of brick. Uncle Rufus walked over to a corner. "Here's a noose," he said. "Just hangin'."

Experimentally, he pulled on it. Without a sound, a section of the wall in front of me swung open. We looked at each other and walked through.

Dust hung in the air. I sneezed a couple times. We had come into a vast, corridorlike room. Cobwebs hung like silk streamers. The floor was piled with refuse—planks and garden tools and long, rolled-up pieces of carpet, and several enormous wooden chests, locked, as I discovered.

"What is it?" I asked. Uncle Rufus walked down the wide corridor, picking his way over the junk strewn everywhere. "Moose heads," he mumbled, looking over the vast array of odds and ends, "Wolf skin, there's an old-style typewriter, and that's a Depression-glass punch bowl. Hmm, look at those racks."

I walked after him. He was looking at some kind of wooden racks. "For wine bottles," he told me. "Like in a wine cellar."

On the other side of the racks, there was a high bookcase, full of odds and ends. We found old clothes on the lower shelves, and then I got up on Uncle Rufus's back to see what was up higher.

"Uncle!" I exclaimed.

"What do you see?"

"Guns! Old ones like in that book you have!"

Right across the very top of the bookcase, someone had wrapped old curtain material around what was obviously a gun. I pulled it down and let it drop to the ground.

"Careful, Jean!" he exclaimed.

"Sorry." I dropped down and unwrapped the material. "It is!" I exclaimed. "It's a musket, just like the other one!"

"We're under the hunting lodge!" Uncle Rufus said. "I thought I recognized some of this stuff. We've come all the way through the mountain to the hunting lodge's old wine cellars!"

"That's right, old man." A light fell on us. We stood up quickly.

Uncle Rufus put his arm around me. "Turn the light down so we can see you," he said. "We're unarmed."

The light was pointed down, and I saw three people standing in the gloom. One was the hermit. One was a woman I had never seen before, and the other man was also a stranger. Uncle Rufus spoke to the woman. "What's a reporter like you doing on someone else's property?"

"What's a preacher like you doing here?" she asked.

"We didn't realize until just now where we was," he said.

"Well, preacher, we'll be sure to see that you get a decent Christian burial," she said.

He held onto me even tighter. "Why?" he asked. "What are you so scared of? Who are you?"

The hermit spoke up in his high voice. "Take them out—out to the river a few miles from here," he suggested. "I don't want anything done on the family property."

"That far?" she demanded. "And in daylight?"

"*Family* property?" Uncle Rufus asked.

"*You're* Angus Maclaran?" I asked.

"Smart girl. I'm sorry you won't be making it to high school," the third man said.

The hermit—Angus Maclaran—looked at me. "I'm used to being anybody I have to be," he told me. "Don't let the hair and beard fool you. As for the voice, well, a little Sunday school girl like you would hardly understand things like fights with broken bottles. Let's just say I was injured, a long time ago. In the throat. I was lucky to have a voice at all when it was over."

Uncle Rufus started forward, and instantly Angus Maclaran and the woman drew guns on us.

"So it's all a lie," Uncle Rufus said. "But why hurt us—why hurt her?" (He meant me.) "She's just a little girl. She can't interfere with that business about the will."

The fake hermit burst into a high laugh. "The will!" he exclaimed.

I knew they weren't going to let us go. So I said, "It's the jewel, isn't it? You're the three that stole it."

Chapter Twenty-seven
Bruce

"There's a shorter way out of here than through the tunnel," Angus Maclaran said. He spoke to the other two. "Take them up through the house."

"We'll be seen," the woman objected.

"Go through the woods. The car is at the usual place. Take a short drive with them to the river and be back soon. They won't put up a fuss. I know their type."

"This little girl's my niece—" Uncle Rufus began.

"Oh, shut up!" Maclaran said. I hung on to Uncle Rufus.

"Don't," I said to him. "I'm all right."

"That's how you got through the house then," Uncle Rufus guessed. "Through the tunnel. That's why there wasn't any sign of a break-in."

"Go on," Angus Maclaran told them. "Get them out of here."

They started herding us up the stairs, when all of a sudden the portable lamp that they had brought down with them went out.

Uncle Rufus acted fast and switched off my head lamp and his. Then he knocked me down, just as one of the guns went off.

"Stay down," he whispered.

"Get them, get them!" Angus screamed.

"Don't do it!" another voice commanded. "You're caught! It's too late!" A light came on—a strong searchlight beam that flooded us all with light. It was hanging up—from the racks, it looked like—and in front of it was a man's silhouette—a man holding a rifle to his shoulder, ready to fire. It was trained on the three thieves.

"Don't try it," he said. "Those peashooters might be good for scaring old men and little girls, but this will take care of all three of you. Drop the guns or shoot your way out!"

Their guns weren't even fixed on him—or on us. The woman and man dropped them. "Hands up!" the newcomer said. "You two on the ground—get their handguns."

We did.

"Good," he said. "Keep those guns trained on them, because this thing I'm holding sure doesn't work." And he lowered it.

Uncle Rufus, concentrating on the three thieves, wouldn't spare himself a look at our rescuer, but he said, "Who is it? It sounds like Bruce Maclaran!"

I switched on my headlamp. Bruce switched on the portable lamp again. He got the three thieves up against the wall with their hands on top of their heads and relieved Angus of another pistol. "It's me all right," he said. "I stumbled down the steps in time to hear Jean say she had found the musket. But these three were ahead of me, coming up right behind you, so I stayed hidden in the dark until I heard everything else happen. Once they started moving you away toward the stairs, I sneaked in and got the musket, then put the light behind me so they couldn't look at me very steady." He wiped sweat off his face. "Don't know whether it was brave or stupid, but it was now or never."

"You knew about this place?" I asked him.

"No. I went up to the cave earlier to try to catch you two and tell you I was sorry about how my Dad acted this afternoon—him being so gruff and all. Your aunt had told me you'd gone to explore a new passage; so I brought my searchlight along to help, but I couldn't find you anywhere. Then when these three showed up, I followed them, and they led me right to the new passage."

He went back through the clutter as though looking for something. "What about these three?" Uncle Rufus asked. "We got to get 'em out of here without any tricks."

"Give me a minute," Bruce called. "These here rolls of carpet are laced up with twine. We can use that. Here I come."

He came gingerly back up the cluttered floor. "This should do it." He used the twine he had cut from the carpet to tie the hands of our former captors. "Let's go upstairs, but I want to bring that musket with me, too."

He retrieved it, and this time it was we who herded them up the stairs.

We took them up over the hill and to the farmhouse. They were a pretty angry threesome, especially because Bruce had tricked them with a gun that wouldn't even shoot. Angus Maclaran called Uncle Rufus a lot of names, but Uncle Rufus just kept saying, "Oh, save it for the judge."

"What I'd like to know," Bruce said, "is where the jewel is."

"Got to be down there somewhere," I told him. "The police will find it."

"And," he added, "I'd like to know how these three knew about that tunnel."

"I can answer that," Uncle Rufus said. "When the will of your great-uncle was stolen from his lawyer's office, there were several letters and other private papers stolen. I reckon your great uncle had wrote a private letter to your father, tellin' him the secrets of the house and other personal things maybe, that related to the family. Ain't that right, Angus?"

But Angus Maclaran was sulking and wouldn't talk to us anymore.

We got to the house and called the sheriff's department, and they came out and picked up the three of them and listened to our story. Then we called up Hugh Maclaran. All that talk about stolen wills had given me an idea. I went out front and found a nice slender branch from the shade tree, peeled it, and came inside.

Aunt Bessie was fussing with coffee and alternately fussing over Uncle Rufus and Bruce, and then, me again, when I came back in.

"I have an idea," I said. "Remember I saw Angus with that other musket, right?"

Uncle Rufus nodded.

"Well," I told him. "Angus knew that the muskets were the favorites of his brother Hugh. And he knew that his uncle had known that, too. For some reason he went looking for the muskets, but he only found one of them. The other one, we know, was hidden downstairs, all wrapped up in a curtain and left with a bunch of junk. But it's here, now."

"Sure," Uncle Rufus said.

I took the musket from Bruce and poked the twig into its muzzle. "So maybe Angus had guessed something that we should have guessed a long time ago," I said. "Everyone knew that there was probably more than one copy of that will; they just had to find one. But Angus and Hugh's uncle would have hidden it in a place he thought Hugh would figure out really fast—in one of the muskets that they both prized so much!"

I scraped around with the twig, and heard it scratch paper. With a little effort I managed to slide a yellowed paper up out of the barrel.

"The will!" Bruce exclaimed. With gentle fingers he slid the wide document the rest of the way out of the muzzle.

He opened it up and read part of it. "Yes, this is it! And Dad's on his way over! This is terrific!"

"And just think," Uncle Rufus added, "all that time Angus was looking for it, he was within a few feet of it!"

Chapter Twenty-eight
The Story Ends

The police still had a hard time finding the jewel, but in the end they convinced Sally Carr, or whatever her real name was, to tell them where it was hidden. It had been in the moose head.

There was a reward for the recovery of the jewel, and I wanted Uncle Rufus to have it so that he could keep the farm going. But he put half of it in trust for me and said he'd manage just fine.

The Maclarans wouldn't take it because Hugh Maclaran said he was in our debt too much and really owed us a reward for finding that will. He told me he was sorry he hadn't believed me about the hermit's being in the cave. He was an awfully gruff man—even he admitted it—and he said it was because life had treated him so hard. Uncle Rufus said he didn't know how a man with a string of stores under his ownership could say that life had been hard. But in any case he did soften up some and even came out to church a couple times to hear Uncle Rufus preach.

Bruce and I became friends, and pretty soon Robbie got envious enough that he at least acted normal so that he could be with us. Uncle Rufus did finally let me go hiking with them.

But my last few days at the farm I didn't go visit the Maclarans much. I was up every morning at dawn to help with chores, and then after the breakfast dishes were done, I would saddle up Sarge and go riding on him, just to feel the horse under me and think about how much I loved him, and what a good and kind horse he was. In the afternoons I would play with the dogs before doing my work in the garden, and every night after supper the three of us, Uncle Rufus, Aunt Bessie, and me, would sit out on the porch eating pie or ice cream and talking.

I wasn't an Indian or a knight of the Round Table. I was just Jean. And I'd decided that I liked chores and cooking and gardening a lot more than I liked adventures and caves and cellars and jewel thieves. I was grateful that I hadn't lost my head when those thieves had talked about "taking us to the river." I'd looked danger right in the face, but I knew it wasn't the kind of thing I would like to make my hobby.

One morning while I was out riding, I stopped up on the hill to watch a car turn into the winding drive. It was our station wagon. It was Mom and Dad. Suddenly all the homesickness I had never felt came rushing in on me. I wanted to see them more than anything.

I brought Sarge around and headed down that hill at a gallop. He came to a sliding stop right at the front yard, and I dismounted in a hurry.

Next thing I knew I was hugging Mom, and Dad was saying, "Is this our Jean?" Then he hugged me and kissed me, and Aunt Bessie and Uncle Rufus came out on the porch as everybody else piled out of the car.

"Where's Penny?" I asked.

"Having adventures of her own," Dad told me. That's all he would say about it. Mom told me I would hear more about it on the way home.

I helped Aunt Bessie make a big dinner that night, and for the last time I went to bed watching the beautiful sheer curtains playing in the breeze. Early the next morning it was time to go home.